Arrival in the Stars

Arrival in the Stars and Other stories

by
Jean Rameau

Translated, annotated and introduced by
Brian Stableford

A Black Coat Press Book

Visit our website at www.blackcoatpress.com

ISBN 978-1-61227-627-4. First Printing. June 2017. Published by Black Coat Press, an imprint of Hollywood Comics.com, LLC, P.O. Box 17270, Encino, CA 91416.

TABLE OF CONTENTS

Introduction

L'Arrivée aux étoiles (Essai vers l'au-delà) by Jean Rameau, here translated as "Arrival in the Stars," was first published in Paris by Librairie Plon in 1922. The shorter stories accompanying the novel in the present volume are all taken from the author's first short story collection, *Fantasmagories, histoires rapides* [Phantasmagorias: Rapid Tales] (1887), published by Paul Ollendorff.[1]

"Jean Rameau" was the pseudonym of Laurent Labaigt (1859-1942), who was the son of a farmer, and was born in the village of Gaas in the department of the Landes, in the south-western corner of France. He retained a very strong affection for the Basque region, as is very evident in *L'Arrivée aux étoiles*. He studied at the Collège de Dax and was employed for a while in a pharmacy in Mont-de-Marsan before moving to Paris in 1880 in order to follow his literary vocation, considering himself a "spiritual son of Victor Hugo," even though he always represented himself in the city as primarily and essentially a "peasant." His choice of pseudonym led to his sometimes being confused with the similarly-named Jean Rameau (1852-1931), a master bellringer, shoemaker and writer of songs; the latter was visited at his

---

[1] Translations of six more stories from *Fantasmagories*, including all the items of futuristic fiction featured therein, can be found in the Black Coat Press anthology *The Mirror of Present Events and Other French Scientific Romance* (2016), ISBN 978-1-61227-486-7.

home in Berry in 1911 by the English poet Percy Allen, who might not have realized beforehand that he was not the author of the poetry collections bearing that signature, but published an enthusiastic account of him in any case.

Like most of the writers of his era, Laurent Labaigt's first ambition was to be a poet. He won a poetry competition organized by *Le Figaro*, and his first two books were the poetry collections *Poèmes fantasques* [Odd Poems] (1883) and *La Vie et la mort* [Life and Death] (1886). When he moved to Paris and became "Jean Rameau," he immediately joined Émile Goudeau's literary club the Hydropathes and subsequently became a regular at the *Chat Noir*. It was in that period that he wrote the stories collected in *Fantasmagories*, which represent one of the more exaggerated developments of the *conte cruel* genre favored by many of the clients of the café. His tales are extreme both stylistically and thematically, combining the cynicism and irony definitive of the subgenre with grotesque black comedy. Although his work has obvious affinities with that of such luminaries of the *Chat Noir* as Jean Richepin and Alphonse Allais, both of whom he would have seen performing there frequently, it has a distinct element of southern bombast in it that makes it distinct.

As is often the case with writers who participated in the literary explosion of the Parisian *fin-de-siècle*, Rameau's poetry generally made use of a great deal of fantastic imagery, and embodied a world-view that exhibits an exceedingly strong affection and quasi-pantheistic reverence for nature, a tendency particularly evident in such collections as *La Chanson des étoiles* [The Song of the Stars] (1888), *Nature* (1891) and *Les Féeries* [Enchantments] (1897). His novels, on the other hand, made use of such language in a purely figurative sense, and tended more to the Naturalistic school of Émile Zola than to the Symbolist school that was often falsely regarded as its rival during the 1890s. His first novel *Le Satyre* [The Satyr] (1887) is steeped in fervent contemporary "decadence" but is entirely naturalistic, as is *Possédée d'amour* (1890; tr. as *Possessed of Love*), whose title, more accurately understood than it was by its English translator, might stand as a description of many of his works, which routinely feature characters "possessed by amour" whose affliction inevitably leads them into extravagance and difficulty, although the novels the author produced in profusion were soon conscientiously adapted to popular taste, becoming a trifle bland in the process.

Throughout the 1890s Rameau wrote copiously, usually publishing two novels a year and numerous short stories in periodicals, the great majority of which remained uncollected, as was not unusual for prolific writers of short fiction; his later work in that vein seems to consist mostly of vignettes of rural life. In 1900 he returned with his wife and only son to live in his native region, at Pourtaou in the commune of Cauneille, where he had bought a farmhouse in 1898, when he reached the height of his fame in Paris. His productivity slowed down after 1907, and his gradually waning literary career was then drastically interrupted by the Great War; his son was killed at Verdun. He spent the rest of his life at Pourtaou, tending in his later years to representing himself as an eccentric and solitary recluse, although he was actually famous in the region and considered to be one of its most notable residents, and his wife did not die until 1935.

At Pourtaou, Rameau diversified from literary work into various other artistic endeavors, including painting, sculpture and—most especially—photography. He apparently maintained an extensive posthumous correspondence with his son, writing to inform him of all the modifications he made to his house, which he gradually transformed into an elaborate and ornately-decorated villa in the Italian style. It was there that he eventually died, although his literary productivity petered out some ten years before then, unsurprisingly, given that he was well into his eighties when he died. He had built himself a monumental tomb, the Gloriette, at the top of a hill, which became famous, although it has now fallen into disrepair; he was not actually buried inside it as he had intended, but at the foot of the hill.

L'Arrivée aux étoiles is a product of the aftermath of the Great War, as its brief preface declares forthrightly, and it deals directly with one of the widespread psychological effects of the war: a resurgence of interest in spiritualism occasioned by the deep need felt by many people to believe that the loved ones who had been slaughtered during the conflict were not entirely lost. Rameau had always combined a strong interest in the fantastic with a hard-headed rationalism, and his interest in spiritualism prior to the war had been conditioned by the conviction that it was essentially a species of intriguing fakery, a conviction expressed in some detail in his novel *Les Chevaliers de l'au-delà* [Knights of the Beyond] (1905). The loss of his son in the war, however, planted seeds of doubt regarding his former cynicism, and *L'Arrivée aux étoiles* is essentially an exploration of those doubts, and an attempt to work through them in a hypothetical fictional case-study. It is a deeply personal novel, although its quasi-autobiographical elements are carefully transfigured in order to accommodate the plot and, in particular, its imaginary heroine.

The novel is haunted by a curious kind of ambiguity, dramatically sharpened by the epoch and circumstances of its production. It gives the impression of trying with all its might to be credulous, while laboring under the long-established burden of the author's habit of treating all such ideas with relentless skepticism and sarcasm. Like almost all of Rameau's novels it is a study of "possession" by an amour that leads its victims into a dangerous impasse, but it takes that particular torment further than any of the other examples in his work, and thus has to seek a more extreme "solution" in terms of its plot and the philosophical conclusions that it is eager to draw therefrom. As a work produced and framed in deadly earnest, it contrasts strongly with the breezy black comedy of the stories sampled from *Fantasmagories*, produced in a very different frame of mind, but the acuity of that contrast not only helps to illustrate the philosophical tension under which the author was working but also illuminates certain common threads of conviction and fascination that even that Great War had not contrived to sever.

Rameau was in his sixties when he wrote *L'Arrivée aux étoiles*—older than the protagonist of the novel, although the beard he always wore appears from contemporary photographs to have been less spectacular—whereas he had written his "rapid tales" in his twenties, and the best years of his adult life had elapsed in the interim, so a modification of his psychological and philosophical outlook would have been only natural in any case. His exuberance would have mellowed, and so, in all likelihood, would his cynicism. He could not, however, have traveled so far internally without the poison that

11

the war injected into his soul. He fought that toxicity with all the psychological weaponry with which his literary art supplied him, as many of his peers did, and *L'Arrivée aux étoiles* is one of the battles he fought in the process, as he sought to raise himself from the deep depression into which the war and his son's death had cast him.

Rameau is primarily remembered today as a poet, and those of his novels to which some value is still attributed generally attract it by virtue of their celebrations of the landscape and culture of the Basque region. It is, however, arguable that he never did anything again as spectacular as *Fantasmagories*, and that the works therein were simply too original and too flamboyant to attract the critical attention they deserved, and still warrant, as crucial contributions to the development of the *fin-de-siècle conte cruel*.

Although *L'Arrivée aux étoiles* contains something of the regional interest that still attracts some attention to his work, it is also of interest as an extended *conte philosophique* seriously addressing the question of life after death as it was conceived at the time by scientifically-enthused psychic researchers, and as it bears upon human psychology under stress. The juxtaposition of the first set of texts with the short novel is undoubtedly a trifle odd, but there was a time in his career when the author was a great enthusiast for oddity and eccentric juxtapositions, and he would surely have approved.

The translation of *L'Arrivée aux étoiles* was made from the London Library's copy of the Plon edition. The translations of the short stories were made from the copy of the second Ollendorff edition of *Fantasmagories* re-

produced on the Bibliothèque Nationale's *gallica* website.

Brian Stableford

Nerehitchahihohihoum! Zi! Zi!

1

Atchoum! Atchihoum! Aratchihohuhoum!

The sneezing of the poet Phidias Dupont graduated thus, rhythmically sonorous, in the copious cold in the head that had transformed his olfactory apparatus into cathedral gargoyles, for twenty-four hours.

The poet sensed naiads in his nose.

Atchoum! Atchihoum! Aratchihohuhoum!

"Why!" he remarked, suddenly. "That's a verse of the new school. Exactly eleven syllables...and how symbolic!

Aratchihohuhoum!

Soon, however, after a delirious *aratchihohuhoum*:

"Eh! What if it were *that?*

That meant the new voluptuousness, the ineffable sensation of future amour, for which Phidias Dupont had been searching for a long time.

Explanations:

2

Nature, thought Phidias Dupont, *opposes herself to the reproduction of sufficiently perfected species. A herring, a primitive and rudimentary being, can give the light of day to a million herrings. A man of genius does not reproduce, or hardly at all. Woman, who is the summit of creation, suffers in order to give birth more*

15

than any other terrestrial mother. One already senses there the resistance of Nature, which refuses to bring modifications to what she has produced of the most intelligent. A day will come when, the human species being perfected, Nature will judge that any attempt at amelioration is futile and when, having exhausted all her creative forces in the embellishment of one species, she will strike the majority of human mothers with sterility.

On that day, how will the last humans, the supreme geniuses of our race, make love to one another?

There will doubtless no longer be the vulgar and henceforth useless amour of ancient times. Beings as refined would find such trivial sensations, in which so many gross and inartistic species indulge, repugnant.

It will therefore be necessary for Amour, the supersublime Amour of the ultimate times, to choose less banal means, and a seat less profane.

Firstly, what will be that seat?

There lay the problem.

3

Now, after a vertiginous *Aratchihohuhoum!* That he had just emitted, Phidias Dupont no longer hesitated. The new revelation had been made to him.

That divine seat was the nose.

4

What an enjoyment, in fact, is that procured by a savant sternutation in the delicate nostrils of an initiate! What amorous hiccup, what spasm of sensual voluptuousness is worth as much as that inappreciable second of

16

dazzlement, that fugitive instant of bliss, in which it seems that the entire being dissolves, deliquesces, evaporates and is elevated to paradise in a sensation of replete felicity?

O elect nostrils, pink nostrils with tender and passionate mucus, you alone will understand the beautiful humanitarian dream of Phidias Dupont.

5

Certainly, the poet's nose was an elect nose.

Delicate and slender in stature, colored with fashionable nuances, constituted of supple cartilages, endowed with delicate lobes that palpitated with the slightest breath like the two wings of a quivering turtle-dove, it blossomed in the middle of the face, splendid and sweet to behold, like a marvelous flower of amour.

"It's me who ought to be the initiator of that new voluptuousness!" Phidias said to himself. "It's me who will be the Messiah of that religion!"

He set to work.

6

After two years of what he called "nasiculture" he achieved the possession of miraculous nostrils that procured him frenzied enjoyments. It was no longer *Aratchihohuhoum!* That he launched in the sternutatory spasm but *Nerehitchahihohihoum! zi! zi!*: an Edenic sigh that he emitted with tremulous lips, a bewildered heart and white eyes; a sigh of the soul falling into languor, and during which his entire body quivered voluptuously, as if beneath a cataract of stars.

Phidias thought: *I'm ready now to evangelize the masses*.

He commenced.

7

The Word was poorly welcomed by the governing classes. Phidias Dupont found himself threatened with Bicêtre, the modern Golgotha.

Oh, the happy times, those when persecutions came to make the advertisement of new philosophies! What is Géraudel himself by comparison with Nero?[2]

Phidias only found one apostle: his *valet de chambre*, an insignificant negro with an extraordinary nose, which one divined to be predestined.

"It's necessary to give an example to the populace," Phidias said to his negro. "I shall marry."

"But..."

"Oh, in accordance with the new rites, of course."

8

Phidias discovered a chaste young woman of sixteen, Eva, whose hand he obtained. Oh, the sweet virgin! She was very dainty, with her nose of dreams, which

---

[2] The reference to Géraudel is to advertisements, familiar at the time as colourful posters, for Pastilles Géraudel, offered as a treatment for the relief of coughs and catarrh. They were the invention of the pharmacist Auguste-Artthur Géraudel (1841-1906), and the posters and postcards he employed in their extravagant promotion still have some reputation as works of art imitative of the designs of Toulouse-Lautrec and Mucha.

was velveted internally by a blonde down. Blonde! Almost curly!

And Phidias blushed before that candid nose, which the young woman displayed ingenuously, all pink and stark naked, with the innocence of beautiful marble statues that do not know what they are exhibiting.

Before making his choice, Phidias had seen, of course the troubling noses of marriageable young women: delicate, delicate noses...enormous, enormous noses...sensuously red, shamefully picturesque or viciously trogoniferous noses...!

But none of them had produced an effect on him as sovereign and as irresistible as the one he had felt before Eva's nose...

Oh, that thunderbolt nose!

9

And the evening of the marriage, Eva's mother having wept superabundantly on her daughter's neck, and the latter having been prepared by tender maternal revelations of all sorts of mysterious and terrifying things, Phidias, whose heart was beating as if to burst, took his white bride by the hand.

The moon was rising over the horizon. The nightingale...etc...etc...

"Eva," stammered Phidias, solemnly, Madame your mother has doubtless talked to you about..."

"Yes, Phidias!" stammered Eva.

And her nose turned pink.

Phidias could no longer retain himself. He took his virginal other half in his arms, drew her toward two soft seats that were facing one another near the window, before the great starry sky; then, having opened a laurier-rosewood box he revealed two little odorous wands of a rare and heady species. The upper extremity of those wands was ovoid, and discreetly granular. The base was surrounded by precious gems.

The first cock crowed in the bright night.

"Oh, Eva!" sighed Phidias

And, offering one of the wands to his spouse, he presented his inflamed nostrils; trembling with emotion, sought with his other wand the palpitating nostrils of his bride, and then...

Let us draw a veil.

10

Nerehitchahihohihoum! zi! zi!

That was still heard in the nuptial chamber when the skylark sang.

11

And a fortnight later, Phidias Dupont, the happiest of men—according to the rite of the future—was walking pensively toward his dwelling, his heart filled with singing thoughts.

That, then, is the formula of the future amour! And it's me who will have the glory of inaugurating it! Vision of hope! Sublime transformations! Where are the anguishes, the troubles, the innumerable woes provoked by the ancient amour? Disappeared with it! All dispersed!

And through his virile nose, Phidias sensed the music of Meyerbeer passing.

He went into his house.

Atchoum! He heard in the distance of his apartment.

The voice of his wife!

Atchihoum! Aratchihohuhoum!

"Depraved!" murmured Phidias.

But he heard an exceedingly lush and well-known sternutation.

Nerehitchahihohihoum! zou! zou!

Phidias shuddered.

"What does this signify?" he said, going pale.

With furtive steps, he headed toward the room from which the suspect sternutations were coming.

"Wretches" he cried, entering it like a cyclone.

Deceived!

His wife and his negro were making one another sneeze reciprocally with the conjugal wands!

12

He threw the negro, his unworthy and abominable apostle, out of the door.

As for his wife, tragically, as was befitting, he said to her: "Madame, you're going to die!"

And he got ready to blow out her brains.

But he reflected soon enough about the blindness of terrestrial justice.

"The bourgeoisie won't understand me!" he said to himself, throwing away his revolver with a shrug of the shoulders.

Oh, but he required a vengeance, though: an exemplary vengeance, a terrifying vengeance that would give satisfaction to his outraged honor!

He launched himself toward his wife.

But he loved her! He loved her, in spite of her sin, the wretch! He felt it keenly, on seeing those pink, fascinating—oh, so pink and so fascinating!—nostrils!

So?

So, to satisfy simultaneously his vengeance and his amour, he made a grim but slightly sadistic determination with regard to his wife.

He ate her nose.

13

Since that day, Madame Dupont bears on her stigmatized visage a magnificent silver nose that her unhappy but inflexible husband has made her affix to it.

It is said that she finds some consolation in the practice of illicit and unconscious amours—of the ancient formula—but the poet lives above those prejudices of another age.

Solitary and inconsolable, he spends his days in a rustic pavilion that he has had erected in the middle of an island.

From there, passing navigators can sometimes hear a languorous and complicated sigh that can be divined, alas, to be uttered by an ashamed and enfeebled voice:

Nerehitchahihohihoum! zi! zi!

Phidias is amusing himself.

Gnu!

Prologue

At the Jardin des Plantes.

Two parallel rows of animals, separated by railings.

First row (sheltered and comfortably accommodated, evidently because of the superiority of the animals composing it): lions, hyenas, tigers, panthers, bears, etc.

Second row: humans.

Those two categories of animals gaze at one another reciprocally with a mutual curiosity.

In one particular location, a group in the human row is extraordinarily amused by making a bear perform capers. For that, the human is throwing hazelnuts at the bear.

For its part, the bear is prodigiously amused by making a human throw hazelnuts and making him utter grunts of an irresistibly comical sort. For that, the bear is performing capers in front of the human.

In brief, they are having an enormously good time on either side.

1

Suddenly, the animals of the second category (humans) turn round, break up and agglomerate with all kinds of typical exclamations:

"What is it?"

"It's over there. Come and see."

Two animals of their kind, two women, arrive at a run, one after the other. Those subjects constitute what is known, in the language of animals of the second category, as a "daughter of the people" and a "loose woman."

The loose woman is pursuing the daughter of the people with guttural cries that constitute a very animated song.

"Stop her! Grab her!" she yelps.

"What has she done?" yelp the chorus of humans in their turn.

"She's just thrown her child in the Seine!"

At these words, all the animals of the second category precipitate themselves toward the daughter of the people, vociferating. The latter is doubtless conscious of having committed something monstrous, for she dare not look at the faces of her peers.

"Why have you killed your child?"

"Because I didn't have what was necessary to enable it to live."

With that, the loose woman utters a mewl of indignation, to which the humans respond in chorus.

Two agents of the police arrive; the young woman is seized, and, in the midst of the jeers of the audience, is taken to the Depot, perhaps to hear herself condemned to death a few days later, for the law—something majestically incoherent, imagined by the animals of category number two—punishes certain kind of infanticide with death.

It appears that the fashion employed by the daughter of the people is one of those.

And during the arrest, a magistrate who happens to be passing addresses lively felicitations to the loose woman, in the name of Justice.

Now there is in that crowd of animals (still number two) an individual male who is a philosopher, and whose reflections have the pretention of going further than the Code.

That individual says this to himself:

"They're going to kill that daughter of the people who prevented that child from living, and they're congratulating a young woman who defrauds people and whose métier consists of refusing life to all the children she might be capable of producing; that isn't just!"

And, revolted by the satisfaction of that kept woman, who is strutting triumphantly in the middle of the men, he goes toward her and, fortified by the logic of his reasoning, he says to her:

"You know, Madame, that if there were any Justice in this world, you would precede the woman you have just had arrested to the Court of Assizes!"

Great hubbub in the crowd.

The bears, the panthers and the hyenas hear prolonged yapping emanating from menagerie number two, the menagerie that the solicitude of the State causes to file past their eyes every day.

There is mingling and jostling. Some of the biped animals take the side of the loose woman, others that of the philosopher. Bizarre howls intersect in the air.

"He's right!"

"However…"

"What about gallantry, Messieurs, gallantry?"

Briefly, a Persian lion, which is dying of boredom at the monotonous spectacle served up to it very day, interrupts its yawning and gets ready to open an eye.

Finally, the loose woman, jeered and whistled, decamps. And, disgusted by the inconceivable principles of those people, in order to regain her composure, she enters the palace of monkeys.

And the rabble of idlers acclaim the philosopher, who, with the modesty of a spirit of justice, bows humbly and then slips away from the ovations.

3

Meanwhile, a warden of the Jardin, his hands behind his back, contemplates the philosopher with a gaze full of touching admiration.

He knows him, that philosopher! He has seen him a little while ago lurking in the garden of medicinal plants, pausing studiously before a green bush protected by railings.

He approaches our hero with respect and puts a hand gently on his shoulder.

"I congratulate you, Monsieur," he says. "You wouldn't have a cigarette on you?"

"Of course, my dear Monsieur," says the philosopher, touched.

And he puts his hand to his pocket.

But now, green leaves fall out of that pocket.

The philosopher blushes and hurriedly picks up the plants that he has just dropped.

Then the warden folds his arms, in the manner of the victorious Napoléon.

"You're a cheeky fellow, you are!" he cries, looking our man in the eyes. "Where did you get that rue?"

"In the garden."

"To do what?"

The virtuous philosopher who can see further than the Code does not reply.

But his confusion and his anger reply for him: "To do what? Well, to make my wife abort, you damned nuisance!"[3]

4

"Well, if that isn't shameful!" says the revolted warden, telling the story to the magistrate, who is passing by again.

And he crumples something in his pocket, absentmindedly.

5

The perspicacious magistrate, who is well-informed, looks the warden up and down and asks him what he has just bought from the trader in medical supplies at the corner of the quay.

The warden is nonplussed and evasive.

"That? Eh, parbleu! It's for...well, yes, without that she'd make an heir every nine and a half months, the little slut!"

6

"At least I have a tranquil conscience. I have nothing to do with the depopulation of France!" says the magistrate—a great elector, very sturdy—as an aside.

---

[3] The reputation as an abortifacient acquired by rue, also known by poets as "herb-of-grace," is greatly exaggerated, although there is no doubting its toxicity in large doses.

And he goes to join the loose woman, who is coming out of the monkey palace.

7

"Hey, you know, warden," shouts the magistrate, turning round, "it's necessary to take the name of that philosopher and come by my office—the philosopher, you, and you too, Madame—to give evidence in that revolting affair of infanticide."

Epilogue

In the row of animals number One:

The bear Martin to the bear François (looking at the humans): "Gnu! Aren't those beasts curious, François?"

The bear François to the bear Martin (likewise): "Very curious, Martin! Gnu!"

For Virtue

I

Why, having seen some woman throw herself in the water from the Quai de Sainte-Eulalie, did Gabriel Laferrade, a tailor, who was angling at the time, put away his maggots, take off his clothes, dive in a masterly fashion, swim, disappear, search the river, and finally bring the unknown woman back to the bank, safe and sound?

For no reason. For virtue.

It is true that the weather was hot, that a bath in the Garonne could only be an agreeable thing in that season, and there were, up there on the Pont de Saint-Eulalie, the long black eyes of the postmistress, which encouraged Gabriel's action strangely, and finally, in the tailor's mind, very distantly, the thought that the rescue might by crowned by...

But let us stop there; one can sometimes find disinterested actions in the life of a man, if one does not make overly profound investigations. So, Gabriel Laferrade, acclaimed by the fifty idlers that his meritorious action had attracted, was heading triumphantly toward the *commissariat de police*, with the woman he had saved when, something huge and Himalayan, suddenly perceived in the crowd, sent a chill down his spine.

That enormous thing was his spouse, Artemise. At there were at the summit of that living joist two sharp eyes that were saying a great deal about that rescue.

Gabriel turned his head away, went into the commissaire's office, stammered a few explanations with all due modesty, received the felicitations of the authority with the requisite confusion and went home, fleeing, as is appropriate, the ovations of the audience.

Scarcely had be entered, however, than he saw the enormity known by the name of Artemise coming home in her turn. It was not only the gaze but also the mouth of the latter that said:

"Well, Gabriel, so you desire the military medal that much?"

"It's not true!" roared the husband, with the convinced tone that the conscience finds in order to lie.

And, after having broken a table with a blow of his fist, he went out, consigning Artemise to the infernal gods.

No, certainly, it was not for the medal that he had saved someone. And the proof is that he did not ask for it.

Except that he had it requested for him—unknown to him, as is appropriate—by an obliging friend.

2

He did not obtain it, the medal.

"Who did he save?" the obliging friend was asked.

"A woman."

The employee shrugged his shoulders. "But everyone has saved a woman, Monsieur! I who am speaking..."

"How many does he need to save?" he friend hastened to ask, in order to avoid the confidences.

"Hmm! That depends. Half a dozen, at least."

Gabriel Laferrade did not despair. He simply resolved to save the requisite number of women, with the required disinterest.

3

Unfortunately, in Sainte-Eulalie, women rarely drown themselves, and Gabriel, in spite of long stations on the stone bridge, only saw them fall down at long intervals—two or three a year, at the most.

Each woman saved thus represented an average unemployment of five months, plus a bout of bronchitis, plus a violent quarrel with Artemise; and you will agree that a second class medal is very little to compensate a lifesaver for so many inconveniences.

It was, therefore, undeniably the virtue.

4

It is true that the village of Sainte-Eulalie had a public garden, a delightful little public garden with goldfish and pink nannies and chubby children, and, well, when one is decorated…eh! eh!

"Well!" cried Artemise, when she learned that her husband had saved a third woman, "so it's to be appointed warden of the public garden that you're so determined to get that medal?"

"That's false!" vociferated the virtuous Gabriel.

And he was again obliged to go out, in order not to do any damage.

After all, even if it were in order to become a warden, what did that prove?

Warden: a ridiculous employment, which does not provide a living. But in order to save a single woman, was he, Gabriel Laferrade, not risking his life every time?

That is virtue, I tell you, nothing but virtue.

And Gabriel, his conscience tranquil, continued to await the obliging desperate individual, under the bridge.

6

A fourth woman fell from the sky one winter morning.

The Garonne was almost frozen. In spite of all his virtue, Gabriel hesitated.

One seeing the red lantern of a tobacconist's shop gleaming in the distance, however, he made one of those heroic movements familiar to operetta tenors and dived in.

This time, Artemise remained pensive.

"Well, well," she finally revealed, after having plunged the green flame of her sharp eyes into the very depths of her dear man. "So you also need a tobacconist's shop?"

The rescuer uttered a cry of rage, and fainted.

7

Gabriel was ill for a long time. Delirium seized him every day, and his desiccated lips then released cataracts of absurd words: *virtue, medal, cross of bravery, Prix Montyon* and *caporal tobacco*. All of that terminated with an: "It's not true! It's for virtue!" that was capable of breaking windows.

He got better, however, Artemise having been obliged to absent herself for a fortnight.

On returning to Sainte-Eulalie, Madame Laferrade found him back on the quay, at his observation post.

It was a spring day. In the sunshine, the trees in the public garden were wearing their beautiful green robes for the first time, brand new and very correct, as befit municipal trees. It felt good to be alive. The Garonne, white with light, was singing very soft airs against the black piles. One might have thrown oneself in for the pleasure of it.

Gabriel waited. He waited for a month, two months, a year.

Nothing.

8

He grew thinner.

"Are they going to make me stand here much longer?" he asked himself, casting an anxious gaze over Sainte-Eulalie.

The obliging friend renewed his request when the national festival arrived.

"How many times have you been refused?" he was asked.

"Three times."

"We can't do anything for you. It's never granted until after four refusals."

Gabriel learned thus that he still had one person to snatch from certain death and one more refusal to endure.

The refusal was granted to him on the first of the year, but the rescue made him wait.

Summer, autumn and winter passed; spring brought the trees back into flower. Never a single suicide attempt.

It's a spell cast by my wife, Gabriel thought.

He made a novena in order to ward it off.

Vain prayers. The Garonne continued flowing, without a single cadaver.

"They have a grudge against me around here!" the rescuer cried. "They only let me live to give me pain. Brigands!"

He showed kindness to all his acquaintances and rendered their life comfortable, hoping to soften them.

Illusory cares. The trees turned yellow again; the Garonne swelled up with autumnal rain; never a suicide on the horizon.

"Deny that there's a crisis, then!"

And Laferrade sensed himself becoming a reactionary.

9

He voted against the government from that day on. Things did not get better.

The virtuous Gabriel became pale and lost sleep.

He had nightmares, and then fits of sleepwalking.

Mute and pale, with long phantasmal stride, he wandered along the Garonne. He prowled the deserted quays for a while, gazing at the water with empty eyes, extended his arms and, vertiginously, plunged into the river in search of imaginary drowning victims.

Oh, the drowning, the clusters of the drowning, the heaps of the drowning that he captured thus, that he brought back to the bank and made to file, white-faced and grateful, before the dazzled eyes of the administration! Oh, the medals, the heaps of medals and crosses that suddenly weighed down his breast and which covered him fabulously from head to foot like a triumphal armor of gilded scales...! *Tobacco! Tobacco! Who wants packets of tobacco!*

But suddenly, a frisson. Oh, the cold!

And Laferrade woke up in contact with the water, in contact with the mild, placid water, white with moonlight, alone!

10

One night—it was the end of the month of March—on awakening like that on the edge of the water, he had a terrible vision.

Heavens! But yes! From up there...splash! Something has fallen in the river...something that moves, floats, and disappears... Finally!

He launches himself forth, swimming; he launches himself heroically, as always, cleaving the black water with his feverish arms. *Hup!* One more effort and there it is, the unexpected victim!

Gabriel advances a hand...

"Oh, that idiot!"

A burst of mocking laughter on the bridge and a shadow fleeing.

It is a dead dog that the rescuer is holding. The April fool trick of a practical joker.

"Oh, it's like that!" grumbled the virtuous Gabriel. "That's all right!"

And a Machiavellian plan suddenly loomed up in his brain.

"Yes, we'll see if...*huh!*"

He stopped. Virtue only seemed to be playing a secondary role in that.

"Let's think about it, though. That young woman, what if I make love to her? Of course! Yes, I'm going to make love to her!"

So he made love to her, deceived her—oh, the human heart, you see!—and waited confidently under the bridge.

Despair! She hanged herself, the deceived young woman, instead of throwing herself in the water.

Youth is very depraved nowadays.

11

Meanwhile, Artemise prospered. Her husband's disappointments caused her to prosper. She grew fatter, became as round as a quail. She had a fashion of saying: "Well, Gabriel, it's not going well any more, is it, the drowned women?" that gave Laferrade crises of epilepsy.

"Pardon me! It's going to make progress!" he riposted, one evening, with fulgurant eyes.

"Oh? How's that?"

"You'll see."

Important repairs were being made to the Pont de Sainte-Eulalie. A central arch had collapsed.

Five or six laborers were working on it. Every evening, one of them put up barriers and then lit red lanterns at certain places dangerous for passers-by.

Bleak and pensive, his body agitated by nervous frissons, Laferrade followed the works with a haggard gaze.

From time to tell he leaned his elbows on the parapet and, somber and taciturn, making pessimistic rounds of the water and spitting in the Garonne, lost himself in considerations of virtue.

12

One evening, he approached a workman. His entire being was tremulous.

Something grave was evidently in preparation in Laferrade's life.

"Come here!" he said, in a low voice, with a sound of chattering teeth.

The workman advanced prudently, worried by the yellow gleams passing through the rescuer's eyes.

"It's you, isn't it, who puts the barriers over the holes every night?"

"Yes, that's me."

The yellow gleams in the rescuer's eyes appeared to become a conflagration.

"Well, what do you want of me?" asked the workman.

In vain, Laferrade coughed, opened his mouth, swallowed his saliva, searched for words; nothing came out.

Shrugging his shoulders, the laborer was about to go away when the hand of the rescuer retained him by the sleeve.

"Well...well...," Gabriel articulated, painfully, his exorbitant eyes seeming to want to pop out of his head, "five hundred francs for you! Five hundred francs if to-night, you don't put anything in front of *that*."

With a vibrant finger, he indicted a hole in the middle of the bridge: a large and gaping hole that allowed the water to be seen beneath it.

The workman understood. It was him who would be responsible for any accidents that might happen.

"Never!" he said, with a fine impulse of virtue. "You'll understand that...that...it's worth more than that!"

13

But the two of them went into an inn. A few moments later, the bargain was concluded.

The tailor promised the workman a thousand francs—all he possessed—and the workman, for his part, promised not to put any barriers or lanterns in front of the hole. The two parties to the contract would spent the night on the bridge, on watch; and only when a pedestrian had fallen in the water would Laferrade give the thousand francs to the workman, from hand to hand.

The two men emerged from the inn, exchanged a loyal handshake, and Laferrade, his heart in paradise, saw a star emerge in the sky, as round as a second-class medal.

14

What a night! An unforgettable night!

It was a dark, moonless night. Gabriel and the workman tucked themselves away in a night watchman's hut, not far from the hole, and them, with oppressed breasts, they waited.

People go to bed early in Sainte-Eulalie. Passers-by were scarce.

Every time a human silhouette approached, Laferrade felt his heart swell within him, like a balloon. The silhouette grew, became a man or a woman, arrived at the hole...

Good! Here it is, then, the terrible moment.

Not yet.

The silhouette avoids the gulf, keeps going, goes along the parapet, and disappears.

Ten times, twenty times, thirty times over, the rescuer had that poignant anxiety. And no one ever fell.

Nine o'clock chimed in the belfry of Sainte-Eulalie.

And more passers-by only showed themselves at long, long intervals.

The Garonne sang against the piles. The workman yawned, becoming drowsy.

Laferrade gazed at the stars, with the expression that Joshua must have had when he stopped the sun.

15

Did they stop?

What is certain is that immediately after Gabriel's gaze, a black form came on to the Pont de Sainte-Eulalie.

Laferrade was no longer considering the stars.

The form continued approaching, became a woman, took the middle of the bridge, marched toward the hole...

"Holy angels!" stammered the rescuer, his hair bristling with anguish.

...marched toward the hole rapidly, and lost its footing!

"Help!"

A cry in the night. Then—*splash!*—the fall of a human body into the water.

"There's your thousand francs!" said the rescuer to the workman.

And, taking off his clothes, heroically, with a long sight that must have permitted the stars to resume their progress on high, he threw himself in the water.

16

Oh, beneficent, voluptuous, revivifying water! His supple body cleaved through it and swam toward the human form.

Out there, she was out there, she shouted, she sank up...disappeared!

This is the moment! Gabriel judged, who, as befit a self-respecting rescuer, wanted to make the value of his intervention felt.

The moon rose.

He dived, searched, and found the unfortunate woman, brought her back to the surface with his customary skill, and was getting ready to tow her, safe and sound, to the bank, when...when...

No! The pen refuses to describe that horrific spectacle!

Oh, the grimacing face of that person, suddenly recognized in the moonlight!

Laferrade uttered a loud cry, a great cry of desperation that must have woken up many sleeping couples in Saint-Eulalie, and, terrified, allowed the person to fall back to the river bed.

He could not save her! No, he could not, the unfortunate fellow!

It was his wife.

17

One does not recover from such catastrophes.

Gabriel Laferrade regained the bank, and, in shock, shivering, his teeth still chattering under the horror of the situation, he started wandering along the quays.

He considered, the moon, the stars, the Garonne, and then, in the distance, on the other side of the river, the public garden. Oh, dreams! Oh, twists of tobacco!

He thought about the thousand francs, wasted, about his consummate ruination, the impossibility of paying for another drowning victim, and, uttering a supreme roar, he threw himself into the water, into the water for good, yes, into the Garonne, head first, into the vast Garonne, into the luminous Garonne, which, ironically, seemed to be ferrying toward the distant sea, myriads of crosses and yellow medals distributed by the moon.

18

But an hour later, a naked and shivering man rang the doorbell at the *commissariat de police* in Sainte-Eulalie with all his might. He was holding his head in one hand, that man, and, with the other, he was hugging himself, as if he were afraid of escaping himself.

It was Laferrade.

"I've got him! I've got him!" he cried, in a shrill voice.

"Who?"

"A desperate man who tried to drown himself. Fortunately," he remarked, "I fished him out in time!"

The commissaire's eyes widened.

"I asked you who!"

"Myself!" said Laferrade, widening them further.

The two men looked at one another for ten seconds without being able to explain their reciprocal bewilderment.

19

The commissaire kept the rescuer until morning and, at sunrise, labored by a suspicion, secretly ordered a gendarme to put on a show of throwing himself in the water.

Solomon could not have imagined anything better.

Laferrade did, indeed, start swimming, seized the gendarme, brought him back to the bridge—and did not ask for any recompense! Finally, it was for virtue!

There was no doubt about it: he was insane.

He was immediately taken to a sanitarium.

The Dilettantism of Crime

1

Jehan Racca, crossbowman, engendered Hugues Racca, master apothecary.

Hugues Racca, master apothecary, engendered Urbain Racca, surgeon.

Urbain Racca, surgeon, engendered Frédéric Racca, restaurateur.

It was therefore natural that Frédéric Racca, restaurateur, engendered a son who, summarizing within himself all the professions and aptitudes of his ancestors, exhibited special dispositions for the voluptuous art, fertile in exquisite emotions, of exterminating his fellows. So there was only one cry of approval, from the Rhine to the Pyrenees, when Hyacinthe Racca, the scion of that illustrious race, was elected master executioner of the beautiful land of France.

2

The first time that Hyacinthe Racca operated in public on some criminal who had killed for the vulgar pleasure of stealing, the habitués of capital executions could not help clapping their hands.

Hyacinthe Racca, to be sure, announced himself as a remarkable virtuoso of the guillotine. In spite of the emotion inseparable from a debut, he commenced with a masterstroke.

Correctly clad in black, with a white cravat and polished shoes, he arrived on the scaffold, bowed slightly to the enthusiasts, without emphasis as without false shame, with the ease of genius that is conscious of its value, passed his hat and gloves to an aide, took the condemned by a slender hand and, tipping his man over, rapidly, with the slickness of a conjuring trick, he introduced the head into the fatal semicircle. That was done in the blink of an eye, before the amazed audience had time to realize it.

Then, gravely, after two seconds of solemn immobility, like a punctuation mark, Hyacinthe placed his left hand on the head of the condemned, set it delicately at the required point, like a hairdresser greeting ready to curl his client's hair, and then, serenely, while he sensed ten thousand ecstatic gazes upon him, he raised his right hand and brought the thumb and index finger together like a dandy offering a flower. Here a further punctuation mark, that holds the respiration of ten thousand breasts suspended—and then Racca brushed the mechanism of the guillotine with his two perfumed fingers.

Snap!

With lightning velocity, the heavy blade fell.

A shiver of enthusiasm made the crowd vibrate.

"Bravo!" cried the audience.

And the applause redoubled when the severed head was seen to make a half-rotation and reappear, suspended by a hank of hair, at the end of Hyacinthe Racca's triumphant hand.

3

After that, the dramatic matinees known as executions became exceedingly popular.

All Europe wanted to see Racca sat work.

The latter always operated himself, and every time with a new mastery.

The executioner, possessed by his art, only lived for the guillotine. Between two executions he grew thinner, his eyes became hollow, the spleen of bloodshed took possession of him, and one felt that that artist of genius would have died rapidly if he had not killed someone every week.

Like Raphael, Racca had several styles. To begin with, he had sectioned the condemned between the second and third vertebrae, which gave an entirely round decapitated head. After numerous studies, he was led to slice the necks one vertebra lower down. In the basket, such heads had more character, more lines, and resembled the effigies of ancient medallions.

In the second place, he had begun by slicing obliquely, with a hint of whimsy. But in correcting his game, he became classic, like all great geniuses, and no longer cut other than correctly, in a plane perpendicular to the vertebral column.

All that was appreciated by the dilettanti, and the judges hastened to send Racca as many men condemned to death as possible, which brought back a little gaiety to the land.

4

But the wisdom of nations has said it: glory and grandeur often doom men.

They doomed Racca.

Having a great deal of worldly success, the young and already glorious executor of noble works was enthusiastic to go to a rendezvous implored of him by a sentimental great lady on the eve of an execution.

Racca, habitually so sober, allowed copious draughts to be poured for him by the hand of the enchantress—with the result that, when the hour of the execution arrived, the executioner was still guillotining bottles of champagne.

Hastily, he mounted the scaffold. No one had the idea of asking the indulgence of the public for him.

It was sickening.

The blade fell maladroitly, as if unhooked by a profane hand, and the head fell, cut at an angle, with half of a fractured jaw.

When he had sobered up, Racca shuddered.

He curbed his head, devouring tears of shame, and, having the sentiment of the ignominious outrage to which he had subjected his art, as decency demanded, he handed in his resignation.

It was rejected.

Hyacinthe Racca insisted.

Humanitarian societies expressed pleas demanding the retention of the heroic executioner in his noble functions.

It made no difference. Racca was unshakeable, and a successor had to be found.

5

O nostalgia of murder!

Three months later, Racca was dying for want of people to kill.

He had an idea, just in time.

He married, was deceived by his wife, and killed the adulterous spouse along with her lover, with all sorts of criminal refinements.

His health improved slightly.

Having been acquitted, naturally, Racca reestablished himself completely by killing a few people in duels.

Then, as he found himself at the head of an immense fortune originating from legacies offered to him by admirers of his talent, he spent everything he had in perpetrating artistic crimes, always bearing the stamp of the greatest originality.

He killed thus several examining magistrates among his friends, without ever getting caught.

Having attained perfection in murder, he resolved to sign his works henceforth. He adopted for a monogram two thrusts of a dagger in the heart of his victims, two dagger-thrusts puncturing the skin at a distance of two centimeters and converging on a determined point in the left ventricle.

One night, in the folly of inspiration, he killed an entire family like that: the father, the mother, the three children and the two domestic servants.

Wonderstruck by this work, he signed all the cadavers, took paper and charcoal, and drew the scene of carnage from memory, on the very location of the crime, before escaping via the chimney-flue.

On that occasion Racca deployed so much verve, so much variety, so much exuberance and lyricism, that the frightful slaughter merited being called, by competent men, the masterpiece of murder.

Racca was dizzied by it himself.

He stirred up the terrorized crowd the next day, and, seeing floods of human heads around him as far as the eye could see, he cried with all his might:

"You're seeking the author of all these terrible crimes, aren't you?"

"Yes, yes!" howled three million voices.

"Well, set up your triumphal arches! It's me!"

6

He was condemned to death.

He marched to the scaffold with a light step on the morning of the fatal day. Except that, seeing that his successor was a banal executioner, devoid of the sacred fire, Racca suffered horribly, and nearly fainted.

At a given moment, no longer able to contain himself, he made a supreme effort on the seesaw on which the executioner had extended him with a prosaic and trivial hand, and, crushing his unworthy successor with a scornful gaze, he roared: Bourgeois!"

And, striking an academic pose, Hyacinthe Racca gave the public a gracious salute, lifted his right hand with a movement full of majestic amplitude, and, brilliantly and artistically, with all the virtuosity of which he was capable, he guillotined himself.

The Phantom House

1

Oh, that great white and square house, brand new and completely empty, in the populous quarter!

It was a luxurious construction of six floors and four staircases, sited, no one knew why, at La Chapelle. Splendid and comfortable it would soon have been yawning lamentably for a year via the sixty-four openings in its façade: stark black openings, all devoid of curtains and bearing on their window-panes the vague 8s traced in chalk that are the stigmata of apartments virgin of tenancy.

TO LET…TO LET…TO LET…

Sixty-four times that insidious appeal was legible on the deserted house. And never—without anyone having any more idea why—was any of those signs removed, except by the wind.

In that phantom house lived, solitary and peacefully, Madame Fleurant, concierge.

The mild-mannered Madame Fleurant had once pulled the cordon in an old house, leaning and vaguely bulging, in the neighborhood of Les Halles.

She had lived for twenty years, happy and honored, in that crowded building inhabited from top to bottom.

But the expropriation was pronounced, the building demolished, and Madame Fleurant had to seek new lodgings for her homeless penates.

It was the new house in La Chapelle that she had found.

Oh, thrice abominable day!

2

At first, it was almost nothing: scarcely a mute anxiety, the internal disturbance that precedes great catastrophes.

Oh, it would certainly be rented, little by little...

And Madame Fleurant polished the metalwork, swept the entrance and scrubbed the stairways conscientiously, as if forty tenants had risked breaking their legs thereon every day.

But after a few weeks spent in that Sahara, Madame Fleurant became morose.

Would no tenant ever come? Never?

None came, ever.

And the nostalgic porter lost sleep for no longer having to pull the night-cordon, losing her appetite for no longer being able to read the tenants' newspapers over breakfast, lost health and joy for no longer having to complain about the dogs in the house fouling the staircases.

It was terrible.

Madame Fleurant grew thin. Oh, the good old days! Oh, all the sweetness of the life of yore! The post arriving every morning, the feuilletons savored during the chocolate, the contents of the letters weighed by the foreside, the postcards read aloud by the smallest in the family. And all that: newspapers, letters and cards subsequently engulfed in Maman's pockets and forgotten there in a profound sleep! Oh, the piquant chats with the domestics! Oh, the rents one collected, and those one

50

didn't collect! And all the rages that overtook you against naughty boys, against parrots, against sewing machines, against the shady conduct of the little lady of the entresol, eh! And the one on the fifth, staircase B! Tee hee! And then, at night, when everyone was asleep, the joy, the ultimate joy, while snoring, of hearing the carillon of belated tenants, and the ineffable, the paradisal voluptuousness of pulling the cordon slowly, in a dignified fashion, at the sixth ring. Ha ha ha! Oh, life, life!

3

Three months, six months, ten months passed.
Never anything.
The proprietor lowered the price.
Sterile effort.
He doubled them
In vain.
The phantom house seemed to frighten passers-by.
An intrepid monsieur dared to venture as far as Madame Fleurant's door from time to time. "Have you an apartment to rent, Madame?"
Gentle irony.
Madame Fleurant picked up four bunches of keys.
"But of course, Monsieur!" she clucked, with her most ceremonious voice.
And for a hour, she towed the imprudent visitor through the empty house, detailing all the lodgings for him, unlocking all the doors, opening all the cupboards, turning on all the taps.
"Very good. I'll come back...," said the patient, alarmed by the solitude of the spectral house.

And he fled, very pale, reminiscent of a man who has almost been buried alive.

"It's no longer a life!" cried Madame Fleurant, one day. "It's necessary to put an end to it."

She summoned her eldest daughter: Isabelle Fleurant, a young woman of sixteen and a half, a model of grace and virtue—an angel—and conversed with her.

An hour later, Madame Fleurant stood up, radiant, a sun in her face.

"Well, you'll permit him to come, your musician!" she said to her daughter.

The next day, a thin fair-haired young man made his entrance into the lodge, flanked by his father and an aunt,

The father jabbered, in conventional terms, a marriage request, specifying that he was soliciting the hand of Mademoiselle Isabelle Fleurant for his son, Amédée Bardusse.

At that point, Madame Fleurant quit the Voltaire armchair in which her peers have the custom on enthroning themselves, and in a solemn voice that betrayed the violent state of her soul, she said:

"Will Monsieur Amédée allow me to choose the apartment that he proposes to occupy with my daughter after the marriage?"

"But of course!" stammered the grateful Amédée.

"That's good."

Madame Fleurant turned to her daughter.

"Be happy, my angel, she sighed.

Then, overflowing with emotion, she put Isabelle's hand in Amédée's.

The eve of the contract arrived.

"You desire something in the eight hundred franc range, don't you, my darlings!" cooed Madame Fleurant.

"That's good. I have exactly what you need, on the fourth overlooking the courtyard. A genuine jewel of an apartment."

But the fiancé had gone pale.

"Oh, my God! What's the matter?" cried Madame Fleurant, running to her bottle of smelling-salts.

The young man straightened up.

"Then…then…," he said, his eyes flamboyant. "It'll be…here?"

"But…"

"And you'll be…at the same time…my mother-in-law and my concierge! Oh!"

And the musician departed, never to reappear.

The two women uttered a great sigh, and then fainted.

4

It was impossible, therefore, to have a tenant, one alone, by the greatest means, even by the sacrifice of a daughter…an angel.

Madame Fleurant, having come round, stood up.

Her eyes were shining with a wild gleam. In a corner of the lodge, Isabelle was weeping.

Mechanically, she embraced her, cut off a lock of her hair, and went out, unsteadily.

She bumped into someone in the corridor, someone heading toward the lodge…but what was the point?

Madame Fleurant drew away.

The sun was shining. She went along the walls, gasping, feeling all her entrails splitting in dull internal rips.

Yes, it was to the Seine that she went: to the Seine, in order to throw herself in. Why live?

She hesitated on a boulevard. Into which place on the Seine should she hurl her miserable remains? Saint-Ouen? Or Paris?

She found an equal distance between those two points.

She decided on Paris and climbed into an omnibus funereally—into the interior, to protect herself from the sun.

She got off at the Châtelet.

She wandered, sinister, along the bank. She approached a bridge.

Horror! The water was dirty!

And the sun descended, and disappeared; then night fell: night, the triumph of concierges.

And through doors that stood ajar, Madame Fleurant saw placid colleagues lighting their gas on the stairways. They all seemed happy, those concierges. They had plump faces, confusedly aureoled. Some were already closing their doors and saying silly things to children who had just rung for the fun of it. Others, tranquil and dignified, were favoring their digestion in a chair, getting up respectfully to salute the people who came in, or greeting them with a familiar nod of the head, according to whether they were a "first" or a "fifth floor back."

Finally, black shadows were perceptible here and there in the solitary streets, immobile shadows beside closed doors, their fingers on the button. *Brrring-brrring!* One divined the electric bells inside, and the grave stance of the concierge waiting for the second ring to open up, as is befitting at nine o'clock in the evening.

Then there was a downpour, which swept the people away and made Madame Fleurant shiver. And the *brrring-brrrings* redoubled at the doors then, provoked by the impatient hands of tenants soaked to the skin.

And Madame Fleurant glimpsed, inside, the calm porters nestled in their armchairs, waiting patiently for the third ring to open up, as is fitting after ten o'clock in the evening.

And a mortal sadness drowned Madame Fleurant's heart then. She walked at random through the streaming streets. She walked, unconscious of the route she was following, paying no heed to the rain, careless of the hour, only asking herself where she was going to die.

And suddenly, she surprised herself, with her finger on a doorbell, in the process of ringing.

She raised her head. She was at home, in front of the phantom house of La Chapelle.

"It's there," she said to herself, her teeth chattering, "there that I ought to die!"

Her daughter opened the door on the fourth ring—it was evidently eleven o'clock—and Madame Fleurant, like a shade, entered into the glacial immensity. She opened the door of the lodge. Nothing, Isabelle was sleeping tranquilly. The unexpected blasts of the bell had not troubled it. Fortunate youth!

Madame Fleurant lit two candles, took a sheet of paper, wrote her last will, and then, drawing herself up to her full height, cast a fascinated glance at the cordon hanging to her right.

"That's it! I'm yours!" she said to it, in a hoarse voice.

And the porter made a noose at the extremity of the cordon and, tragically, placed it around her neck.

Brrring!

A ring!

"Someone having a joke," muttered Madame Fleurant, blowing out the candle.

And, her neck in the noose, she kicked away the stool on to which she had climbed, and then swung in the void.

But then a cataclysm occurred.

Great gods!

Someone came into the house. Someone for whom Madame Fleurant had opened the door, without intending to do so, by hanging herself with the cordon.

And that someone—vertigo!—cast a sonorous name into the stairwell, and then went up.

"Am I dreaming?" expressed the already-bloodshot eyes of the hanged woman.

And she agitated violently, sticking out an immeasurable tongue, along the wall, in the dark.

"Maman? You've come back?" asked the thick voice of Isabelle, who woke up.

Then solemnly: "There's a tenant, you know!"

"Heavens!"

"Yes, someone came as you were going out, who took two rooms on the fourth and moved in right away."

"Ah! Ah! Ah! Ah…!"

There was a hectic clamor in the darkness, a clamor that made the whole empty house tremble and made Isabelle's hair stand on end.

The young woman struck a match, trembling.

God! What did she see! Her mother, in convulsions at the end of a rope, like a long strangled cat.

She bounded forward and cut the cordon.

"Oh, my daughter! my daughter!" sobbed Madame Fleurant, hugging her child to her bosom.

And, saved, invaded by hope, resolved to live, since there was a tenant, she dissolved in tears of joy.

6

She suddenly interrupted herself.

"Midnight! Quarter past midnight, even!" she said, her face darkening abruptly. "And I opened up to that monsieur on the first ring!"

Then, patting her heavy feather pillow with her energetic palm: "I hope that never happens again!"

And she went to bed with compunction.

To Be Deceived

1

"Monsieur," said the aged and repulsive Edward Spacker to his future father-in-law. "I'll consent to marry your delicious and ravishing daughter, but on one condition."

All the heads and shoulders around Edward took on the contorted aspect of vague question marks.

"What is that condition, Monsieur?" asked the father-in-law, in a shocked tone.

"That Mademoiselle your daughter will sign a document by which she promises to deceive me within the first three months that follow the celebration of the marriage."

2

Edward Spacker, sixty-five years old, correspondent of the majority of the scientific societies of the world, had made the following reflections:

"What is the greatest charm of life? It is experiencing the strongest sensations that it is humanly possible to experience.

"Now, what sensations do I not know?

"I know the sensation of amour; that of hatred; that of drunkenness; that of glory; that of murder—I have killed both as a physician and as a duelist. I have written

58

a book about each of those sensations. What remains for me to experience and write about?

"Ah!" he said, suddenly, touching his forehead. "It remains for me to experience and describe the sensations of a deceived husband.

That is why he got married.

3

Amélia, his fiancée, was very pretty, very likeable, very witty and very poor, and Edward Spacker being very old, very ugly, very prone to catarrh and very rich, the young woman's parents were unable to refuse the old scientist anything, and the aforementioned document was signed by the hands of both parties.

"Madame," said Edward on the wedding night, taking the beautiful spouse to the sumptuous bedroom that he had had prepared for her, "I shall strive to render the task facile for you, and even agreeable. I'm bald, fat, rheumatic and somewhat gouty; I squint with my left eye, and no one can look me in the face for ten seconds without wanting to throw nuts at me as if at a chimpanzee in a fairground. I have charming, witty and devoted friends; I have on good terms with everyone who has made a name in the sciences, acrobatics, finance, gymnastics and belles-lettres; I hope that you will not make me languish and that you will render me the happiest of husbands before the expiration of the legal term."

And so saying, he kissed her hand gallantly, rang for the domestics to come and undress the bride, and went to his study in order to write the preface to his next book.

4

At four o'clock in the morning, his preface concluded, Edward entered the apartment reserved for his wife on tiptoe.

He approached the bed.

"Alone! Already? That's not good," he murmured, with a smile of disillusion.

And, slightly annoyed, he went to sleep in the bed of a bachelor and corresponding member off the majority of the world's scientific societies.

The next day, Edward introduced his wife to an Apolloesque tenor, the most stupid that he could find in the subsidized theaters, and slipped away quietly while his wife and her tenor side by side, we looking at a photograph album on a side-table.

Nothing.

The following week, no less malign, Edward introduced his other half to a hairdresser, and then a contortionist, and then a laureate of the Académie.

Sterile efforts.

Perhaps I haven't given her everything she needs to do her duty, the scientist reflected. And he put successively at his wife's disposition scandalous novels, revolvers, chaste poetry, a can of vitriol and other accessories of modern amour.

Still nothing.

"Madame," said Edward, in a grave voice, "it will soon be three months that we have been conjoined; I am reluctant to drag your name before the law courts, and thus throw dishonor upon your family. However..."

Then, by way of conclusion, he announced in a sonorous voice, while picking up a traveling valise: "I shall not be back for twenty-four hours."

And he went away, with a classic stride, as cuck-olded husband do in theatrical melodramas.

When he came back, two hours later, Edward sur-prised his wife *in flagrante delicto*, embroidering a pair of slippers.

"Wretch!" he roared, with an explosion of anger.

But he restrained himself, thinking that everything would be irreparably ruined if he started beating his wife.

5

He shut his coachman in with her one day, without seeming to be doing anything, and then, breaking a floodgate, he caused the stream in his park to overflow, with the consequence that Amélia and the domestic—an excellent fellow who had lured several dozen comtesses to sin—were besieged by the waters in a pavilion with the absolute impossibility of separating.

The following night, Edward leapt into his boat and rowed feverishly toward the inundated pavilion. There was a light on. O hope! His heart beating as it once had during his first amorous rendezvous, he scaled the bal-cony and went in.

Amélia was having the domestic polish the parquet.

"John!" said Edward to the latter. "Take my boat and never let me see you again."

And, crimson with wrath, after having thrown the dishonest coachman out, he turned to his wife.

"Then you persist, Madame?" he demanded, his teeth gritted.

"Oh, Edward!" sighed Amélia, throwing her arms around his neck.

"That's all right."

Swallowing a tear, he launched himself tragically toward the balcony and threw himself in the water.

6

It was terrible.

Amélia, in despair, plunged into the water after her spouse, but an importunate Newfoundland dog pulled her out.

Then she had the bed of the stream explored by divers and drag-nets.

No more Edward than in her hand.

A week went by.

The flooded park dried out.

Amélia-Calypso etiolated.

On the night of the ninth day, the inconsolable widow, perfectly convinced that her husband was dead, went out, her hair in disorder, uttering sighs in the direction of the moon, and, mad with chagrin, came back in order to hang herself from the balcony from which her idol had thrown himself in the water.

Amélia had already stuck out a few centimeters of pink tongue at the end of the rope when the idea occurred to her to gather all her remaining strength in order to murmur the name of her beloved one last time.

"Edward!" she gasped.

"Here! Here!" replied her husband, suddenly appearing at her feet.

7

Amélia's tongue elongated by a good centimeter more.

"I wasn't dead, darling!" exclaimed the husband, cutting the rope. "I dived, I reached the bank, I spied on you, angel, treasure, model of all the virtues!" he pindarized, while covering his wife with caresses. "Are you not divine, then? Everything I have done thus far, that clause in our marriage contract, that extravagant conduct, those inconceivable demands, my pretended suicide, all that was to put you to the proof, O flower of chastity!"

"Really?" gasped Amélia.

"I swear to you!" proclaimed Edward. "Do you want irrefutable proof of it? Here, look!"

And, with a pathetic gesture, he took the stamped paper on which the famous contract was written, and tore it into little pieces.

"Oh, my love!" sighed the sympathetic Madame Spacker.

And, her eyes overflowing with sweet tears, they fell into one another's arms.

However, Amélia, half-strangled, was dying.

"But you must live!" cried the husband, with a roar like Othello. "I love you; we're going to be happy; you must live!"

Amélia, in seventh heaven, could only hug her husband in her arms.

"Anathema!" howled Edward. "Help! Someone, quickly, to save my wife!"

And, seeing his new coachman—an old groom afflicted with St. Vitus' Dance—come running, he cried: "I'm going to fetch a doctor! Courage!"

And he went out, after having kissed his wife passionately.

Five minutes later. Edward, who had remained on watch, uttered a terrible snigger.

"Finally!" he thundered, in a triumphant voice.

And, opening the door wide, he was fortunate enough to find the moribund in the process of embracing the old coachman.

Amélia straightened up, as rigid as a statue.

And, showing her fists to her husband, who tranquilly started taking notes for his book, her eyes bloodshot, she croaked: "Oh! You've...deceived me!"

And she fell back, stone dead.

Between Friends

1

I have the honor of introducing you to the poet Léonard, a notary's clerk at times.

His portrait, his morals, his political opinions and the name of his mistress?

Why? Limit yourselves to knowing that, having written in secret a poem in fourteen parts entitled "Infanticide," he was striving, at the moment when this story begins, to attract public attention to his work, and had found no better way than this: to pass himself off as an individual who kills a little child every morning between two cigarettes, in order to digest his watered chocolate.

Léonard felt that that legend, adroitly launched on his account, might be useful to him. The court would order an investigation; the poet would be arrested; examining magistrates would find the skeletons of young monkeys in his cellar, and obliging physicians would allow it to be thought, until the day when they filed their reports that those skeletons belonged to infants born viable. All the newspapers, all concierges and all parrots would be talking about Léonard and his infanticides. *Bang!* Publication of the poem! A lived poem! What a scandal! What success! What glory!

"Let's find monkey skeletons and a good denouncer," Léonard said to himself. "The publisher will come of his own accord thereafter."

2

Having found his monkeys, he summoned his new domestic—an excellent fellow, mild and honest in appearance, who was reputed to steal from his masters with a rare conscientiousness.

"I give you good wages," Léonard said to him. "I hope you'll always conduct yourself in my regard as a god and loyal servant."

"What can I do for you, Monsieur?"

"You're going to put the story around everywhere that since you've been in my employ I've killed three young children."

The domestic went pale.

"Monsieur," he said, haughtily, "I'm not what you think."

And he handed in his apron.

In an omnibus office the next day, Léonard felt the hand of a pickpocket who was stealing his watch.

That's my man, thought the poet.

And, taking the thief by the collar, he drew him aside and spoke to him, exactly as follows:

"You're caught. You can save yourself."

"How?"

"By putting the story around that I, Léonard, poet, of 16 Rue de la Tour d'Auvergne, killed two twin children this morning, and that the cadavers, still warm, can be found in my larder."

"Never!" replied the thief.

"I'll give you my watch, into the bargain."

"Never!"

And he allowed himself to be taken to the police station.

4

"Damn! This might be hard," Léonard reflected.

In a drawing room, a pretty girl passed in front of him.

"How obvious it is that she has false teeth," said Léonard, in a loud voice.

The pretty woman had forgotten her revolver. She looked at the poet with a thunderous expression.

"Madame," the latter then said, falling at her feet, "You can render me the happiest of men; tell your friends that I've killed my four children, when I didn't catch anything fishing."

The young woman hesitated.

"No. Two bullets in your breast, if you wish," she replied, condescendingly, "but not that."

5

"Why didn't think of that immediately?" Léonard said to himself, leaping for joy.

And, full of hope, he went to find an escaped convict, an eminent pimp, a forger emeritus, a considerable murderer, suspected at that very moment of having killed one of his comrades and stripped the skin from his cranium in order to make a tobacco-pouch.

"Here's fifty louis for you," Léonard said to him, mysteriously.

"What is it necessary to do, bourgeois?"

"Something serious."

"Poison an entire barracks?"

"Well…"

"Have no fear; spit it out."

"Well," confided Léonard, a trifle confused, "it's necessary to tell your comrades and even a few policemen, when you have any contact with them, that I killed a child a few weeks ago—only one, very small child, who would have died anyway of whooping-cough the next day."

The refugee from justice started.

"Monsieur," he said, in a dull voice, devouring tears of shame, "I've fallen very low, it's true, but to do what you're proposing there…me, an honest murderer, become a cowardly informer! Oh!"

And, with a dignified gesture, he showed Léonard the door.

6

The poet shivered.

If Z*** refuses, I've had it! he thought, with amazement.

Z*** was another recidivist, just as dangerous: a recidivist and an atrocious, implacable personal enemy, who had the added complication of having tried to kill him.

"Don't protest!" he said, on going into Z***'s house. "I've come to furnish you with an opportunity to satisfy your hatred against me."

"You want to die?" asked Léonard's implacable enemy.

"Better than that. I want to be dishonored, stigmatized, dragged away between two gendarmes; last week I killed eighteen unweaned children; you'll find he skeletons in my house, between two casks of claret. Denounce me!"

Léonard's enemy drew himself up to his full height, trembling with anger, and unleashed his two bulldogs on the impudent poet's legs.

7

Léonard was saved by a miracle.

Seeing that he could not put his hand on anyone monstrous enough to denounce him to the law, and not wanting to lower himself so far as to denounce himself, he resolved to die.

He took the manuscript of "Infanticide," reread it from end to end with an affectionate eye, and serenely, after having added his testament in verse and a few considerations on the future of poetry, he got ready to hang himself.

8

But then a fulgurant idea—a marvelous idea, an idea of genius, such as only come in the supreme moments of life—suddenly sprung into the poet's mind, and caused Léonard to utter the most resounding "Eureka!" that any Archimedes ever pronounced.

Léonard had, in fact, found it.

He hid his poem, put the skeletons in evidence, went out into society, took the arm of the mildest, most honest, most loyal and most devoted young man he could find, took the young man home with him, was tender, generous and eager to please him, lent him money, heaped him with delicate cares, addressed him as *"tu,"* loved him—and was finally glad to see a *commissaire de police* flanked by four gendarmes apprehend him bodily, accusing him of infanticide.

The honest and loyal young man had denounced him.

It is true that he was not a lackey, nor a thief, nor a murderer, nor an implacable enemy.

He was better than that.

He was a friend.

A Son of Two Fathers

1

To take a wife for oneself alone, and to keep her for life, is very expensive and tedious.

So one finds many men who do not take a wife at all.

On the other hand, a son is certainly nice, and just as amusing to take for a walk as a dog in an overcoat.

But that can cost even more.

So it is only people without a sou who permit themselves to have children.

What if one were to take a middle course, possessing half a wife and half a child? Or even, in accordance with one's ambitions and resources, possessing a third, a quarter, a tenth or a thirty-sixth of a child and a wife?

2

"Why not?" wondered the ingenious Charles Brouchican, an old bachelor, not very rich but not very poor either, who thought himself ripe for the joys of the hearth.

And, seduced by the idea, he studied that new system of social life laboriously.

3

Six months later, Charles Brouchican and his fervent friend Gustave Jouvenot, correct and dignified, introduced into a house that they had rented in common, an agreeable young woman who responded to the double forename of Marie-Rose

"Mademoiselle," said Charles Brouchican solemnly, having attributed the functions of the officer of the new civil estate to himself, "the Code, in spite of the progress and needs of the century, does not authorize yet matrimonial unions such as my honorable friend and I understand them; that is why I am obliged to fulfill the functions of the Maire personally in our wedding, my respectable friend and co-husband having reserved everything concerning the religious service for himself."

And Charles Brouchican, searching his throat for an appropriately grave voice, said: "Mademoiselle, will you swear amour, constancy and eternal fidelity to both of us?"

"Yes," pronounced the solemn bride, lowering her eyelids.

The three-way marriage was consummated.

4

They were all happy.

Marie-Rose was alternately Madame Brouchican and Madame Jouvenot for the duration of a day, from noon to noon.

She was not bored.

She was faithful to her husbands.

The latter returned the favor,

One called her Marie.

The other called her Rose.

She carried a little calendar in her pocket on which she marked in red pencil the days when she had to call Charles the elect of her heart.

The days when she had to call Gustave that were marked in blue pencil.

That almost always prevented grave errors.

And the household functioned with a perfect regularity, each of the husbands furnishing, in equal parts, money, little attentions, amour and esteem.

Why would they not have been happy? The supreme happiness, as everyone knows, consists of being the lover of a married woman. Each of the co-spouses had only to believe himself the lover of a woman married to his best friend.

That thought alone sufficed to fill them with an unalloyed felicity.

5

A son—their budget did not authorize any more— was born to them one day.

He was named Jean-Pierre.

And each father gorge himself on familial joys, on alternate days.

The child was handsome. Each co-father thought that his demi-son resembled him.

He was spiteful. Each one thought that his demi-son was the moral portrait of the other.

A double consolation that is scarcely permitted to ordinary fathers.

6

One morning, noon chimed. Brouchican quit Marie. In the antechamber he bumped into a fair-haired man who was going in.

Shady!

"But Monsieur, would you care to tell me…?"

He reflected: *After all, it isn't me who is... No, it's Jouvenot, since it's him that since midday…poor Jouvenot!*

And he left.

A short while afterwards, Jouvenot, taking leave of Rose on the stroke of noon encountered another man, this one dark-haired, who was going in.

Poor Brouchican!

Let us add moreover, that they were both decent fellows, and as each of them thought the other blind and ridiculous, he was a good enough friend not to open his eyes.

7

But one day, a terrible event:

Fifteen leagues from the conjugal domicile—they were traveling for common interests—Charles Brouchican and Gustave Jouvenot discovered, on a public promenade, a lovely person who…and whose figure…

In brief, the opportunity, the soft grass, the memory of Marie-Rose also pushing them…

8

At midday, as they were in a private cabinet in triangular company—habit, it is said, is a second nature—someone knocked on the door.

Tap, tap!

The hair of the two husbands stood on end.

"Wretches! Roared Marie-Rose, coming in. "You're deceiving me!"

She aimed a revolver.

9

"Stop, Marie!"

"Stop, Rose!"

"Thank about it!""

"Yes, it's only one of us!"

Thus cried the two husbands.

Very true, Marie-Rose said to herself. She searched for her calendar

Red pencil!

Bang! She fired the revolver at Charles.

But she thought: "What time is it?"

"Quarter past noon.

"And you've been here since..."

"Eleven forty-five," declared the lovable person with the pure figure.

"Deceived by both!" exclaimed Marie-Rose. "Oh, that's too much!"

Bang! She fired another revolver at Gustave.

Then, doubly deceived, doubly criminal, and desirous of a double expiation, she loaded two more revolvers, and missed twice.

10

Charles and Gustave were due to expire the following day

It was Brouchican who commenced.

He summoned his half a son.

"My child," he croaked, "I'm going to die. You'll close my eyes."

Jean-Pierre looked at his watch.

"Papa, I'm only your son today for another seventeen minutes..."

"That's right! That's right!"

And he hastened to die, fearing that his son would only just have time to close his eyes.

A Woman's Heart

1

The races yielding little that season, Georges Crick, a lover of sport, wagered, one day in late summer that he could make any pretty woman that anyone cared to indicate fall in love with him.

The wager was taken, and a charming young widow of twenty-five was indicated to him: Blanche d'Altemur.

2

The next day, Georges Crick, who had the pretention of knowing a woman's heart better than anyone, sent the young widow a little eclectic package composed of flowers, pralines and jewels.

Nothing.

The day after, he sent a wreath of pearls for her husband's grave and a wallet full of banknotes.

Nothing.

"Madame," said Georges Crick on the third day to the interesting widow, I'm handsome, bald, rather stupid, not too bad a horseman, I play the cello, I sometimes have a drop, I've fought thirteen duels, I write sonnets, I have aptitudes for acrobatics and, being rather stout, I offer a certain surface area to discarded women who want to fire revolver shots at me. Reflect, Madame. You'll rarely find as many qualities in a single man.

Nothing.

"We'll have to use the great means, then!" Georges Crick said to himself.

And he reread with attention the poets, dramatists and novelists who were reputed to know a woman's heart like their pocket.

3

He had the widow thrown in the water one night by a refugee from justice in his pay.

When Blanche was at the bottom of the Seine, Georges, who was on the alert, dived, caught up with the unfortunate victim and, by force of devotion and courage, snatched her from certain death.

The window did not offer her hand to her rescuer.

Georges bounded.

"You've never been to the Opéra-Comique, then, Madame?" he roared.

And, illuminated by a sudden idea, he raised his hand against the widow and delivered himself to ignominious ways of action upon her.

Blanche did not make the slightest declaration of amour.

"What, not to the Théâtre de Montmartre, either?" vociferated Georges. "But in what places have you learned to know life, then, you poor thing?"

4

He presented himself at her house one night, very grave and clad in black.

"Adieu!" he said to her, in a tremulous voice. "Think of me sometimes."

Blanche did not reply.

"Ask me if I'm going to fight a duel," Georges whispered, in a low voice.

Blanche shrugged her shoulders.

"Well, yes, Madame, you've guessed it: I'm fighting, Oh, not for you," he added, in a pathetic tone. "I never said that. Adieu! Be happy."

Blanche rang for a domestic to show him out.

"It's too much!" thundered Georges. "I'm fighting tomorrow morning with a scoundrel says that your glove-size is six and three-quarters, and you're not going to throw your arms around my neck to attempt my virtue? That's contrary to all the rules, Madame!"

And he stormed off.

5

Georges Crick was gravely wounded in that duel. He had himself taken to Blanche on a stretcher. Would the spectators at the Odéon have believed it? She did not offer to care for him.

It was in the region of the heart that he had been wounded. A surgeon put a rubber apparatus between his ribs in order to try out on him a discovery he had just made. The duel and that rubber apparatus supplied gossip for a long time. All the newspapers talked about them.

Seeing that the public was avid for information, one of them announced gravely that a rubber heart had been fitted into the wounded man's breast.

The next day a rival newspaper announced that everyone knew that the heart was rubber, but what they did not know was that the heart in question beat with the aid of a clockwork mechanism and that it was necessary to wind it every day.

There was no talk of anything but that, and, with the aid of foreign newspapers, it was son known in America that there as an individual in France whose rubber heart played a tune from *La Mascotte* every time a pretty girl was nearby.[4]

"Well, well!" Blanche d'Altemur said to herself, on reading the details in her newspaper

And, like a host of Englishwomen, Hottentots and Papuans, who proposed to cross the seas, Blanche resolved to go and pay the phenomenon a visit.

6

"No women here!" exclaimed the physician, on seeing the young widow arrive.

"Will it do him any harm, Monsieur?" asked Blanche, with interest.

"The slightest emotion might kill him, Madame."

Blanche had a commotion. Her eyes shone, her nostrils dilated, her breast swelled, lifted up like the bellows of a forge.

---

[4] *La Mascotte* is a comic opera by Edmond Audran first staged in 1880, whose farm-girl heroine brings everyone good luck so long as she remains a virgin. The title was adapted into English as the now-familiar term mascot, although it originally comes from a Provençal dialect term meaning a magic spell or its caster. Although the story does not specify which song from the operetta the imaginary rubber heart is supposed to play, the likely contender is the duet in the first act in which the heroine tells her swain that she loves him even more than her beloved turkeys, while he bleats like a sheep.

"I'm doomed!" she sighed, hiding her face with her hands. "Georges! Georges! I love you!"

And, overflowing with passion, she threw herself into his arms—and waited.

Georges did not die.

His heart did not even play *La Mascotte*.

"Monster!" cried the Parisienne. "You don't love me!"

And she collapsed, prey to a crisis of nerves.

7

Blanche d'Altemur loved Georges Crick madly, furiously, increasingly, even when she learned that her lover did not have a musical heart.

Even when she learned that her amour did not kill that lover.

A woman's heart is an enigma.

She loved him with such an intensity of passion, such obstinacy, and such rage, that Georges Crick became anxious.

It will be very difficult to get rid of her, he thought.

His friends declared that he would never get rid of her.

"What do you want to bet?" said the indefatigable lover of sport.

"Anything you like."

The wager was similarly taken, and George Crick, man of genius as he was, won again.

8

You might perhaps be wondering, Parisiennes, co-
quettes, women, how Georges Crick succeeded in making Blanche d'Altemur fall out of love with him.

Alas, it was quite simple.

He fell in love with her.

The Living Statue

One day, the funereal news arrived:

Rumor has it that the Laniscard Mission has been attacked by the savage peoples of Sudan. The entire column must have been massacred. (English origin.)

Six months later, the news was partly confirmed. A year later, a committee was organized to organize all sorts of benefits for the widow Laniscard.

2

"That Captain Maurice Laniscard, what a man!" one of the friends of the deceased wrote, then.

"A man of talent, who wrote several masterpieces, Monsieur!" riposted another friend.

"What, a man of talent? say rather a man of genius!" exclaimed a third.

And a fourth said: "Yes, of genius, Messieurs, and misunderstood genius. For if Laniscard has embraced the career of arms and departed for Central Africa, it was in a moment of literary discouragement; I received the confidence of that—me, Joseph Nimportequi."

"Let's raise a statue to him!" responded the friends, in chorus.

And the erection of a statue was decided.

3

"Well, well!" said Maurice Laniscard—who was as alive as you or me—to himself on disembarking in Marseille and reading all the details in a newspaper.

4

The captain had only had his nose removed by some cannibal. That gave him a singular appearance, which did not go too badly with his eccentric character.

As soon as he was on land he sought information with regard to the statue of him that was being erected in advance of his final farewell.

A marble statue, if you please, of natural size.

Worthy friends!

They were all on the committee, naturally.

They had all written funeral orations about him; all of them cited his witty quips, and even invented a few.

Excellent friends!

All of them, playing the "Captain Laniscard card" had succeeded in acquiring some status. They published their best works by attributing them to Captain Laniscard; the articles of the enormous poet Z*** or the unctuous critic Y***, articles unanimously rejected by all the periodicals, were accepted by replacing those celebrities' names by the name of Laniscard.

Divine friends!

"It doesn't matter! It's fine!" said the captain to himself, his eyes filled with tender tears.

And he took the express to Paris.

5

In Lyon he learned something terrible. A critic, having dared not to declare Laniscard's works admirable, had been sent two seconds by one of the latter's friends.

The friend had been wounded.

"Ah! It's only the dead who have friends like that!" exclaimed Laniscard, in a fit of lyricism. "What a fine moment for him when I show myself alive and happy, with my arms extended toward all those comrades, to hug them to my heart."

6

Several times, on the way, he had the temptation to send them a telegram.

No, he had reflected, *it's necessary to give them a surprise*.

He arrived. He immediately headed for the house of the wounded friend.

What if the emotion were to kill him? he asked himself.

He turned back and went into a telephone booth. He made contact with the friend in question.

"Are you quite sure that Laniscard is dead?" he asked him, disguising his voice.

"Of course!" replied the friend's weak voice.

"However, according to recent news..."

"Oh, the poor fellow"! He's really dead!"

"But..."

"I'm sure of it, I tell you."

"However..."

"Since I tell you that the savage who ate him assured me that he found him excellent."

Still by telephone, Laniscard wanted to sound out his other friends and let them know that the man they were mourning might well be alive. But all of them were intractable. They would not permit his death to be put in doubt. It was poignant

"Oh, they'll see!" exclaimed Laniscard.

And, as the date of the inauguration was approaching, he resolved to put into execution an idea of genius—and, in consequence, slightly insane—that had occurred to him.

7

It was a memorable day.

A day of sunshine. A day of national reparation.

Oh, spectacles like that one are good for the soul.

At the appointed hour, the committee arrived before the statue of Laniscard, covered with an enormous gray sheet.

They were all there, the friends: all consternated, all dignified.

They all had eloquent and tender speeches in their pockets, of which the reporters had obtained god copies the day before. What an apotheosis for Laniscard!

The members of the crowd already felt emotional and were preparing pocket handkerchiefs. In the meantime, they pointed out to one another the members of the committee, whose names had been published seventy-eight times a day, on average, since the opening of the subscription, and photographs of whom were being sold in all stationer's shops.

And dialogues ran around the pedestal.

"Poor Laniscard! If only he could see all this!"

"Ah!"

Suddenly, the national anthem burst forth, launched to the skies by a thousand singers. And up above, on the virgin statue, the sheet stirred.

8

But then ten thousand cries erupted.

There was no statue on the pedestal.

Or, rather, there as a living statue, a man, an unknown man in a frock coat and varnished boots, contemplating the committee with the stupid and luminous eyes of someone about to weep for joy.

And the statue, unbolted by him, lay on the ground.

"Sacrilege!" cried the crowd, as one man.

And they rushed the living statue, led and directed by all those that the amity of the captain-litterateur had rendered famous, by all those to whom his death had been worth an advancement, by all those who occupied a position that, when alive, he would have been able to occupy.

And Maurice Laniscard, who had wanted to enjoy his triumph and give an original surprise to his former comrades, was booed, whistled, knocked unconscious and then thrown into the water, with a piece of the statue around his neck.

9

He had not been recognized by the crowd, poor fellow.

And he had been, by his friends!

One Does Not Trifle With Honor

1

I have the honor of introducing to you: 1. Monsieur Florentin Barlock, professor of mathematics; 2. Madame Barlock, his other half.

Two scrupulously faithful spouses, honorable and loyal.

So loyal, honorable and faithful that they cannot succeed in making a good household together. They are suing for divorce.

2

It is evening.

The professor of mathematics goes into his wife's room.

She is there.

In the process of being embraced by someone else.

"Anathema!" cries the faithful, honorable and loyal Barlock.

And, taking possession of a revolver, he gets ready to kill the guilty parties and then blow his brains out, as the simplest proprieties demand in such circumstances.

3

But the guilty parties leapt up.

"Stop!" they clamored.

"Why?"

"The divorce has been pronounced!"

"You think so?" asked the husband, becoming perplexed.

"We're convinced of it."

(A moment of reflection.)

"Bah! But in that case…yes, that's true!" said the
husband. "Monsieur, Madame, I beg your pardon…for
having disturbed you…"

And he withdrew, confounding himself in apologies.

4

A few moments later, however, Florentin had a suspicion.

As he did not trifle with the laws of honor, he made
enquiries.

Alas, the result was deplorable.

Barlock found himself obliged to rush upon his wife
and the latter's lover.

"What do you want, Monsieur?" they demanded, on
seeing him come back in.

"To avenge my honor, wretches! You've dishonored me!"

"Impossible!"

"It is as I tell you."

"But the divorce…?"

"Was pronounced at three-fifty p.m. Yes! But the
incriminating act was committed by you at three forty-
five. That clock marked three forty-six when I arrived.
So, I am dishonored! Which was to be demonstrated!"
roared the professor of mathematics, in a tragic voice.

And he prepared to avenge his honor.

5

But the two accused leapt up.

"Stop!" they cried again.

"Why?"

"The clock is slow!"

"Do you think so?"

"By ten minutes. We'll prove it to you."

And it was, in fact, proved.

"In sum…since it's thus," said the husband, "I renew my apologies. Monsieur, Madame!"

And he went out, bowing deeply.

6

But one is not a professor of exact sciences for nothing.

Florentin had a further suspicion.

He went to the courtroom where the divorce had been pronounced.

He went there with a clockmaker.

The courtroom was several leagues from his home in a easterly direction.

Barlock returned to the house, his hair standing on end.

"There's no beating about the bush!" he exclaimed, finding the two accused again, whom he had had kept under observation. "You've definitely deceived me, scoundrels!"

"Really?"

"It's indisputable. The clock in the courtroom was also slow."

"By how much?"

"Six and a half minutes. So...

"Follow my reasoning carefully. By the clock here, three forty-five plus ten minutes late equals three fifty-five, the time which the act for which you are reproached took place, isn't that true?"

"Yes," replied the others, slightly bewildered.

"For the clock out there, three fifty plus six and a half minutes late equals three fifty-six and a half, the time at which the judgment was rendered. So..."

"So?"

"You dishonored me for a minute and thirty seconds!"

"Horrible!" cried the guilty couple, and prepared to die.

And Florentin cocked the avenging revolver.

7

But at the moment when he was about to fire, Madame Barlock uttered a cry.

"A word!" she implored

"Speak, Madame."

"The time here isn't the same as that of the tribunal. We're necessarily a few moments behind."

"Why?"

"Because we're to the west of it."

"That's true."

"Let's calculate that delay."

And the three individuals, with anxious hands, took geographical maps, calculated the longitude of the courtroom, the longitude of the house, and calculated how much time the difference represented,

Al three of them uttered cries.

91

"But then...it was at the same moment that the judgment was made!" exclaimed the husband, increasingly perplexed. "Great gods, what a situation!"

And all three took their foreheads in their hands, to meditate on that extremely serious situation.

8

Suddenly, the husband stood up, his features semi-contracted.

The two accused, astounded, stood up in their turn.

"How long did the incriminating act last?" demanded the husband.

"Hmm...let's say three minutes."

"Three minutes. That's clear!" growled the professor of mathematics, in a semi-grim voice. "There was, therefore, a culpable minute and a half and a half and a licit minute and a half. The entire three minutes constituting the dishonor, one minute and a half constitutes the dishonor divided by two. I'm half-dishonored. I ought to half-kill you and blow out half my brains thereafter!"

"Oh!" clamored the two demi-culpables.

And their teeth started chattering like castanets.

9

"Let's reflect!" the husband went on, whose widened eyes took on a strange expression. "I ought to cut your throats half way through, or—oh, what a mess!—remove one arm and one leg, an ear and an eye from each of you—what a mess!—half a mouth, half a...what a me...me...me..."

"*Me me! Me me!*" replied the other two, uttering the cries of ferocious animals and starting to talk politics.

10

And the next day, all three of them were incarcerated in a lunatic asylum, where they are still reflecting on their horrible and insoluble problem.

ARRIVAL IN THE STARS

Let there be light!

A Few Words, If You Please

For some time, a spiritual tide has been rising, which is pushing humanity toward all kinds of new churches. These churches bear various names—Theosophy, Occult Science, Spiritualism, Metaphysics—but although they have different rites they have the same origin and tend to the same goal. The fervor of their devotees demonstrates that many of us are weary of the dense materialism with whim we have been overwhelmed for a hundred years, and that we are trying to liberate ourselves, to breathe more deeply on higher plateaux. It seems that the reign of matter is ending and that of the spirit is beginning.

It is the war to which we owe that. The millions of men that it has killed are acting upon the living. Their souls are drawing us, and we are trying to renew links with them that an odious fatality has broken. We do not want to admit that they are entirely dead. Of a rose that is no more, a perfume remains in a bottle if one carries out certain laboratory operations. Why should we not succeed in making, for a dear departed, that which we make for a plucked flower?

"Return them to us, at least return something!" cry millions of desperate individuals, raising their arms to the heavens in a gesture of supplication.

And from all directions, one sees the columns of a new religion, which is trying to render them to us. Will it succeed? Its apostles are certain. They declare that we are marching toward the total light, and that the world will be saved again. They profess that it will soon be proven, mathematically, on the blackboard of every school, that the soul is veritably immortal, that it is responsible, and that we ought to be good to our peers if we want them to be to us. On the day when that principle is scientifically established, mores will change and it will be pleasant to live on this planet that has gone astray, where the materialism of the last century is in the process of rendering the civilized people of today more cruel, more ignoble and more stupid that the wild beasts of the jungle.

In this book, which he has entitled *L'Arrivée aux étoiles*, the author has tried to show where the works of the new church are at present. Once, he had not much belief in its definitive edification, since he remembers having published, twenty years ago, another book, *Les Chevaliers de l'Au-delà*, in which he described the underside of spiritualism, occultism and magic, unmasking the faces of a few exploiters of the Mystery, then in vogue. Now, he remains convinced that Mystery has always had its bad priests, but he no longer doubts that there are good ones therein. And he says his prayers for the advent of that new religion, which ought to console and regenerate us.

But he will also be permitted to regret that so many unfortunates have been turned away from the old religion, so beautiful and so pure, and perhaps no less scientific, which has already brought us all the consolations and all the hopes, while advising us to practice all the virtues.

J.R.,
April 1922.

I. Eve's Apples

She is a beautiful young woman. She is blonde and flourishing. She has eyes the color of a dewy meadow, and a healthy flesh with a scent of the harvest. Distracted passers-by would like to put her mouth in their buttonhole like a red carnation. Her smile has the radiance of a rising nascent star. Her name is Eve Illiberri and she is twenty years old.

What do Eves who twenty years old ordinarily do? The eat apples. This one, therefore, will eat apples. She will not fail in her mission. Her name, her beauty and her youth offer her that counsel; and summer imposes it upon her: an exceedingly hot summer, which is harassing the apple trees and exciting them to hasty ripeness.

And indeed, in the orchard of La Floride—that is the name of the villa in the Basque country where Eve is staying for a few days—there is an apple tree whose fruits are already round, perfumed and tempting. What is that delicious variety? Eve does not know. She rarely riffles through horticultural catalogues.

Doubtless one of those pedantic papers would reveal it to her, the name of the puerile apple that has the god taste to ripen first. She would find it in the chapter *Malus*, for scientists have had the Latin insolence to name the divine tree that bears apples *Malus*. (Perhaps that is because they can no longer bite into it.)

But those papers do not interest Mademoiselle Eve Illiberri. She is content with the enlightenment of her gardener.

"Mademoiselle, it's a Saint John's apple tree," the worthy Etchecopo has told her.[5]

And he is right, that man. It is now 24 June, St. John's day, the precise day. And since the apples are ripe, the apple-tree is well-named.

"I wish you a good festival, my beautiful friend," says Eve to the tree.

And her arms hug the furry trunk, familiarly, like the carcass of a genteel ancestor.

Oh the apple tree! Does it not have a scent a little like the roundness of those two other apples leaning on its bark? And its own, less tender, will they not be perfumed up there?

The weather is mild. The first flies are buzzing. There are noisy ones that have blue gleams, as if they had rubbed their wings against the sky, which are carrying out bold investigations around the ripe fruits. Can their probosces be planted therein?

Eve chases them away by agitating her scarf. Those apples are for her, for alone.

At twenty years old, can one imagine that fruits, flowers the sun and all the good things of the earth also belong to others? They are one's own. But the gnat that takes off from a blade of grass needs to believe that the universe was created for it.

Eve picks an apple and eats it, without peeling it, avidly. What heresy it is to peel a country fruit, a fruit that one has detached from the tree oneself! The skin is the velvet, it is the perfume, almost the smile. One might as well scalp the head of a lover before oppressing him beneath one's lips.

---

[5] i.e. *Malus pumilia*, also known as the Joannine apple or the Paradise apple.

Eve Illiberri even swallows the pips. Everything that one loves is good. The tree is vigorous and healthy. It is not one of those invalids of the espalier, pruned into a palmate form, as there are in Northern gardens. It is an apple tree, not of the Empire style but of the terrestrial paradise style. The first man and the first woman must have found one of that appearance between them.

What a pity it is that not the slightest grandson of Adam is visible on the horizon! The granddaughter of Eve would perhaps have welcoming smiles for him this evening, even if no fallacious serpent invited her.

Saint John's Day is the season of fires. In Gascony there is one near every house and in every breast.

Eve's eyes close for a few seconds and her lips part instinctively, as if the charming breeze were laden with kisses. And are there not, in fact, in the wind of certain days, unknown kisses escaped from tremulous, appealing, sighing mouths?

Young women sometimes start to weep, all alone, without knowing why, and it must be because one of those kisses has reached their lips.

Eve does not weep; on the contrary, she starts to sing. But a song almost always signals a heart for the taking. This young woman's does not belong to anyone yet.

"It is only yours, handsome apple-tree," she says, resuming picking apples.

And there is a certain melancholy in that confession.

She feels the apples that are within arm's reach. Not many of them are ripe. In any case, almost all of them are dishonored by the thumbprints of Etchecopo or the maidservants. The gardener's children must also have undertaken investigations, as well as the furry wasps.

But there are beautiful ones higher up! Why is everything that is tempting so high up? Does Nature want to counsel effort, climbing, violence and rape? Perverse!

Eve gazes as the mocking apples that shine overhead, seven or eight meters from the ground.

"Well, I shall have you!" she says, unlacing her sandals.

She will climb the tree. It is no big deal. She's lithe and strong. Like the majority of young women of her society, she practices various sports; she plays tennis and dances.

But she is not content to take off her sandals; she takes off her stockings. Oh, the pleasure of feeling the wind on her bare legs! That above all is what she ought to have: kisses.

She throws her stockings in the air, as a squirrel thrown away almond shells. And one of them hooks on to a branch of the apple tree. That makes a funny patch on the tree, a kind of pink decoration. Intrigued, a cock-chafer comes to investigate.

For some months, elegant women have been wearing short skirts. But if the fashion in Paris is to show one's calves, in the Basque country it is to show one's knees, for everything is exaggerated in the South.

Eve is a Southerner, and her legs are shapely. Why should she not follow the fashion?

Her extra-short skirt is a great help to her in that climb; a boy could not do any better. In a matter of seconds, she arrives at the top of the tree. There she sighs with pleasure. How pleasant it is! What fine weather! She has kept her straw hat, but that also inconveniences her. She takes it off and throws it away. Then she lets her hair down so that the wind can play with it. She has a crazy desire to do that; it tickles the nape of her neck pleasantly.

"Go on, amuse yourself," she says to the wind, taking out her combs.

She knows, too, that she has beautiful hair. Why deprive the cockchafers of the sight of it, its perfume, its gold? And, suddenly finding her sleeves too long, Eve rolls them up all the way to her shoulders.

Oh, how glad the wind must be! It has all of her. Eve feels it on her legs, on her arms, in her armpits, on her back—all the way to her wings, perhaps, for this evening she surely has wings.

"My God! If Madame Hirigoria could see me!" she says, with a burst of laughter.

It is her governess that she names thus. Fortunately, the lady has gone to the market in Bayonne today. There are only the cockchafers to watch over Eve.

How good it is to be free, alone, all alone with the universe! Today, there is nothing to do anywhere: no reception, no garden party, not the slightest dress-fitting. One can stay at home, vagabonding under the trees, read, think, by quiet, get bored. And that is good, from time to time.

But how can one be bored? From the top of this tree she can see so many things: the road that runs alongside the orchard; the cedars of the park; a cow in the meadow; white houses in the green countryside. And that pinch of gray powder over there is Bayonne; and that thread of silver is the Nive; and that plate of glass shining in the sunlight is the sea; and those fragile blue bubbles, which the wind seems capable of bursting with a breath, are mountains.

Eve is tempted to blow kisses to all that, to shout to the four points of the horizon, like a general to a valorous army: "Fields and meadows, towns and forests, mountains and sea, I'm content with you!"

She has the impression that all those things have been created for her pleasure. She admires them, and thus makes them her own. In the distance, in the sharp gulf that introduces itself, like an azure caress, between ocher cliffs, there is a host of blue sails—fishing-boats tacking toward the Spanish coast. Perhaps they imagine, those brave fishermen, that they have set forth to catch herrings or sardines, to make rich hauls at sea and bring home bags of coins, or at least wads of paper? What an error! They have no other mission than to enchant the eyes of a young unknown whose name is Eve Illiberri. And those towns, where so many people are busy; those mountains, where so many flocks are wandering; that railway, where passing trains are carrying a thousand feverish individuals: all of that is nothing but an ingenious spectacle organized for the distraction of one little girl.

At that moment, so much force is seething in that exuberant blonde head that she has the illusion of being all of life, of filling the world and absorbing God.

Each of us has lived at least one of those magnificent hours, and it is ordinarily when amour approaches. Amour, being divine, enlarges proportionately the souls that it comes to visit.

Eve sings and frolics, as unconscious as the blackbirds in the vicinity. She has taken a branch of the apple tree with her left hand and is leaning her bare neck upon it; with her right hand she picks apples. She eats one, two, three. How her teeth sink into their pulp! She thinks about Jean's cheeks, with have a slightly similar odor.

One apple seems to her to be too green; has she not found the same acidity in Georges' smiles? Yes, a few kisses, here and there. And what young woman of twenty has not collected a few of those in the course of her days? But none has reached into her depths, none has truly brought her the juice of a heart.

In the fourth apple that Eve attacks, her teeth sink to the middle at the first thrust.

"Oh, I'm going mad!" she says to herself, grunting with anger, impatience and who knows what.

And, as she is no longer hungry for apples, she contents herself with biting into them and then throwing them away. She bites all the beautiful ones, all the gilded ones, for no reason, for the pleasure of tearing them beneath her gums, of branding them with her mouth, of snatching them from the covetousness of others. By what right would any other living being eat apples? They have only ripened for her, those apples, and those she cannot crunch become useless.

"There! There! There!" she says, between two bites, between two throws. "All for me! For no one but me! Get away!"

She throws them at her hat, at her sandals, at the road. She would like to throw them all the way to the town, to pepper the mountains with them, to fill the sea with them.

Abruptly, however, a cry goes up from the road. Eve turns her head and sees a passer-by.

"Oh, my God! I've hit that man!" she says to herself, ashamed.

She remains motionless in her tree. The man has stopped. He seems old and infirm. He puts his hands to his eyes.

I've injured him! Eve thinks.

She descends from the apple tree, without making a noise, with the ease of a marauding weasel. She says to herself: *It's the scholar, the stranger who goes past every day. I must have hurt him.*

She leaps over the grass at the foot of the apple tree, picks up her sandals and runs toward the boundary wall. That wall overlooks the road.

"Have I hurt you, Monsieur?" she asks, fearfully, leaning over the wall.

The man raises his head. He glimpses that beautiful young woman with semi-naked arms, her hair loose, of whom the setting sun seems to make a golden idol. He picks up his stick and continues on his way, tentatively, without responding.

"Oh, Monsieur, I didn't do it on purpose! Tell me that you forgive me! Monsieur, Monsieur!?"

He does not say a word, and continues to draw away.

Then Eve returns to the apple tree, picks the most beautiful apple that her hand can reach, and starts running along the wall in the direction taken by the man. There is a wooden gate at the end of the wall. She opens it with a push and catches up with the man on the road.

"Monsieur, I beg you to forgive me. I'll be so unhappy if you don't forgive me. I didn't see you. I was throwing apples at random. One fell on you, perhaps in your eye. How I regret it, Monsieur. Will you accept this apple? Oh, I beg you to take it!"

He sees the apple in the bare hand at the end of the bare arm. And he sees the bare legs...

He turns his eyes away and moves aside slightly in order to continue on his way.

But then Eve gets down on her knees in front of him, on the road.

"I beg you...," she says, in a low voice, smiling.

And her two hands present the apple to him.

What can he do? He accepts it. He takes it in his stiff, wrinkled, colorless hand, which, it seems, ought no longer to be touching a single fruit of terrestrial orchards.

"Thank you, Mademoiselle," he says, lowering his eyes.

"Oh, you don't hold it against me anymore! It's me who thanks you."

And she stands up again, patting down her skirt with a prompt hand, in order to lower it slightly, and then curtsies.

"I wish you *bonsoir*, Monsieur. I hope that your eye will be better tomorrow. It's a Saint John apple that I've given you. It's good. Taste it, you'll give me pleasure. And until tomorrow! I'll watch to see whether you go past tomorrow. I'll bring you more apples."

He went away, slowly, leaning on his cane—but he did not taste the apple.

Eve followed him with her eyes. Soon, she saw him sniff the apple. Doubtless he found its perfume agreeable, but he did not eat it.

Ten paces further on, he sniffed the apple again, stopped, and appeared to hesitate for a quarter of a minute. Then he threw the apple on to the road, in the direction of three little pigs being guided by a child. One of the animals ate the apple.

"Oh!" Eve complained, raising her bare arms, as if to summon a celestial thunderbolt.

And, furious, she returned to her apple tree.

II. A Queen Passes By

Jean and Georges, Philippe and René—all the others, her amorous young admirers, sighing magnificently after her—what would they have done if she had offered them an apple?

They would have accepted the apple—and with what enthusiasm! Even if they had been wounded by her, they would have fallen on their knees before her, murmuring her praises. In any case, they would not have thrown the apple to the pigs.

And now that old man, that human detritus, that dust of tomorrow, has had the audacity...

Eve could not calm her wrath.

She put her silk stockings on again, put up her hair, picked up her hat and marched toward the house, crushing the apples that had fallen in the grass beneath her hard feet.

She paused in the antechamber and darted a glance at the mirror. She found herself ugly therein. Every defeat ages, diminishes and stigmatizes.

She dined poorly, went to bed early and slept badly.

The next morning she went to find her gardener in the park.

"Tell me, Etchecopo, you know everybody...what's the name of that old fellow who goes past every evening, dressed in russet like an old shepherd?"

"Dressed in russet? There are several, Mademoiselle."

"No, not like this one. The old man with a beard and long hair, very thin..."

"Ah! The scholar?"

"If you like."

"The one that lives at Larbouset? The madman?"

"Ah! He's mad?"

"So it's said. Some call him the Scholar, others the Madman."

"It's not the same thing, though, Etchecopo!"

"Pretty much!"

"And why do people call him the Madman?"

"He has such funny ways..."

"Such as?"

"He never eats meat; he browses like a goat; he doesn't speak to anyone; he buys calves in the market, then he goes to release them in the mountains; he stands for hours looking at a dandelion through a magnifying-glass; he goes to the funerals of poor folk without even being invited; he's never been seen to drink a glass of wine."

"Really?"

"If Mademoiselle thinks that all that's Catholic..."

"Indeed. What is his name?"

"I don't know."

"Where is he from?"

"I don't know."

"Far away, no doubt?"

"For sure. Perhaps the savage lands."

"Is he married? Does he have a family?"

"Who can say? In any case, he lives alone at Larbouset, like a beggar, which doesn't prevent him from spending hundreds and thousands on lunacies."

"What lunacies? Do you know of any?"

"It's said that he had a house built on the Rhune for an idiot shepherd who has visions and puts flowers of the grave of a dead dog, and many other farces. But if Mademoiselle wants to know him, she only has to watch the road at sunset. He goes past every day."

"I know."

"And I'd be very astonished if this evening, between seven o'clock and half past..."

"Thank you, Etchecopo. He intrigues me, that man. I'll be on the road this evening, between seven o'clock and half past."

Eve went back up to her bedroom. What her gardener had told her lacked precision, but the scholar, the madman, interested her no less. In the provinces, eccentrics are so rare. Life there follows a banal rhythm. Eve liked unexpected rhythms.

At seven o'clock she took a book and went to walk on the road alongside La Floride's orchard.

She had made herself beautiful: a mauve straw hat with a large violet rosette over her right eye—for the fashion was then for women to wear blinkers, like some ill-tempered horses—and a white muslin dress with mauve flowers; mauve shoes and stockings; and an amethyst on her right ring-finger to complete the harmony. Her heels were only eight centimeters. Her skirt only left her legs uncovered as far as the modest relief of the kneecaps, and the neckline at the back stopped in the middle of the back. The fellow had seemed so shocked, the day before, by the bare calves and the loose hair; perhaps he had taken her for a savage. He was about to be shown that she was a young woman of the world.

She had equipped herself with a makila,[6] like an oxherd, and to complete the elegance, she hid her wrists in gloves with soft stems, which tapered and were perforated, like the skin of poorly-scalped Kanacks. They cost seventy-five francs a pair, and the Parisians at Biarritz

---

[6] A makila is a type of walking-stick unique to the Basque region.

came to show them off at the Madrilenas of Saint Sebastian.

But Eve Illiberri's efforts were wasted. The Madman did not go along the road that evening. She only saw Melchior Illiberri, her father, coming. He was arriving from Bayonne in his new automobile, with which he was very pleased: an American model of which his colleagues, the bankers of Bayonne, were rightly jealous. Melchior Illiberi had made three millions in Czechoslovakian loans. He was not sorry to let that be known to his compatriots, the rude Euskarians, all enriched by the war, so inflated by greasy paper that a gust of wind would have blown them into the Atlantic.

Eve received a paternal kiss on the forehead and climbed into the auto in order to return to the house more rapidly.

"You seem sad, Evelyne!" (Evelyne was more chic.) "Perhaps you didn't receive a declaration today?"

"Indeed!"

"What do you think, then, of the gentlemen of our Basse-Navarre?"

"Papa, do you know an old man who lives on Larbouset's farm, near here, on the Arbonne Road, whom people call the Scholar, or the Madman?"

"No. What's the point of such an individual? He doesn't have a deposit at the Illiberri bank."

"I don't think so."

"So?"

"That's true."

The father and daughter no longer talked about any but conventional things: The impending performance of *Phi-Phi* at the municipal casino (it was necessary to go, since the Gomezes has already reserved a box) and the arrival of Her Majesty Queen Christia of Bessarabia, who had come to take up residence, with a staff of fifteen, at the Mondial Palace.

At half past eight, an intimate dinner: twelve guests, and then a few neighbors after the toothpicks. Two or three flirtations for Eve, but nothing serious. Foxtrots and a jazz band. Everybody off to bye-byes at two o'clock in the morning. A Biblical evening.

The next morning, at seven o'clock in the afternoon—as people still say in siesta country—Eve went to walk along the road again, not far from the Saint John apple tree, but in a symphony in blue pastel this time. Would the credit of the Illiberri Bank have seemed solid if the daughter of the house had shown herself in the same costume on two consecutive days?

But the Scholar, the Madman, did not pass along the road any more than he had the day before.

Eve was anxious. Was he ill, by chance?

On the third day, Etchecopo announced to her: "Nothing astonishing, Mademoiselle, if he no longer goes by. He's blind."

"What do you mean, blind?"

"I saw him a while ago on the terrace at Larbouset. I was going to sharpen my tools at the forge nearby. Your fellow had a bandage over his eye and a little boy was reading to him."

"A bandage over his eye? You're sure you saw that?"

"Yes, Mademoiselle."

"Poor man!"

"Perhaps he hurt his face falling, or perhaps he caught a nasty blow."

Eve did not listen to any more. She headed for the garage.

"The auto!" she requested. "The auto for three o'clock."

She inundated herself with the latest perfume launched by the great chemist of the Rue Royale—*Yours for life!*—and departed with her governess in the direction of Larbouset.

It was a large farmhouse with white walls and red shutters, which wooden lattices on its façade, in the Basque style. It stood on the summit of a small hill. To get there it was necessary to turn off the Arbonne road five or six hundred meters from La Floride and then go up a stony, portly maintained road. The auto had a great deal of difficulty climbing the hillside.

Eve cast a glance over the farm. Chickens, ducks, guinea-fowl. A vine, not virgin, over the façade. A skewer of spices and garlic between two chevrons. Through an open door a cow was bellowing. The effluvia exhaled from that door were not *Yours for life!*

"Pardon me, Madame," Eve asked a peasant-woman who was knitting, "you have for a lodger a scholar, a..."

"Yes Mademoiselle. He's upstairs."

"Can one pay him a visit?"

"I'll ask him."

"Tell him that it's the young woman from the other day, who threw an apple at him. I'd be very glad to see him again, if he could grant me a minute..."

"I'll ask him," the peasant-woman repeated, planting her knitting-needles in a cushion.

Two minutes later, she reappeared.

"You can go up, Mesdames. I'll take you. This way. Be careful of that step on the staircase, which isn't properly aligned. There! Duck your head because of the beam. Another little corridor. We're there. I'll open the door for you."

A bright room appeared. Whitewashed walls, an iron bed, two wickerwork chairs. On two shelves a hundred books and pamphlets. There was no one in the room.

"The doctor's on the terrace," the peasant-woman explained. "You can go on. The door's open. Excuse me if I don't go ahead of you. He's not doing too well, the poor fellow."

Eve and the governess went toward the terrace, hesitantly. There was no carpet on the floorboards. Flies were buzzing over the curtains of the window. On the ceiling, trickling water had pointed something like futuristic frescoes.

Having arrived on the terrace, Eve perceived her man. He was sitting in a wicker armchair, his feet in the sun and his head in the shade. He had a woolen blanket over his knees, and on the blanket there was a sheep.

Eve stopped, astonished. But yes, it really was a sheep, a white sheep like those in any sheepfold. And at the slight of the visitors the animal uttered a prolonged bleat, which seemed to say: *Good God, what's this coming?*

Madame Hirigoria, the governess, made a slight grimace. Ordinarily, Mademoiselle Eve did not take her to the homes of people of a different quality.

On seeing the bandage covering one of the old man's yes, however, the young woman was moved to pity.

"Monsieur, forgive me for being indiscreet. I've come to obtain news of you. How are you, since the other evening? Are you really suffering, then? And perhaps I'm the cause of it! How sorry I am! Let me renew all my apologies. I haven't told you, my dear friend: it's me who, by throwing an apple from the top of an apple tree, has injured Monsieur. I didn't want to believe it, but it's necessary to yield to the evidence. Oh, Monsieur, if I could only heal you! Can I do anything for you? Speak, speak!"

He had not yet pronounced a word. On the other hand, the sheep—or rather the lamb, for it seemed very young—was much more loquacious. It bleated and bleated, without respite, in a lamentable voice, which must have been full of alarm and supplication—but his master calmed it down with a flick.

"Shut up, Pascalot!" he said, softly.

Then, turning to his visitors: "There are two of you, Mesdames, it seems to me. I have exactly two chairs in my room. I offer them to you on my terrace, where there is sunlight, and a beautiful view. Contemplation is the final joy. That is all I can give you, but I give it to you gladly."

He tried to get up in order to go fetch the wicker-work chairs, but Eve ran, more nimbly.

"Don't disturb yourself, Monsieur!"

She went in search of the two modest chairs, giving one to the governess and sitting down on the other.

Yes, the view was beautiful: villages, hills, mountains, and a little of the sea to the west. But Eve only looked at the man. How strange, unfashionable and ridiculous he seemed!

He wore a full beard—and could one, since the war, flout convention to that extent? Like all women of her generation, Eve no longer admitted any but hairless, naked faces, shaved in the American style.

If the man had only contented himself with an ordinary beard! He had enough to garnish three or four faces.

The twelve apostles could have been contented with it. The beard descended to the middle of the chest. It covered the neck and the ears. It went all the way up to the eyes and seemed to reemerge through the nostrils.

His attire was no less inelegant: a long russet cape like a Franciscan monk's robe; an upright collar and round cuffs. Round cuffs had not been worm for twenty-five years. The man was judged.

A scholar? No. A feeble mind. Public rumor was right.

"Doctor" the peasant woman had said. Doctor of what? Fossil sciences? Troglodytism?

And he wore no decoration. He had felt slippers on his feet. His long hands, joined over the lamb's fleece, must smell of wool-grease, like those of a shearer. It was not astonishing that the man had thrown the Saint John apple to the pigs the other day; it must have smelled too good for him.

And he dared to look at the mountains and the sea? Did he not fear to stigmatize them?

Eve felt less guilty toward the old man. She had given him a black eye? That was damage, undoubtedly, but really, worse things could have happened. And anyway, she had not seen him very clearly the other day; the setting sun sows deceptions everywhere.

Eve was about to get up after a few banal words when the peasant woman reappeared, carrying a round basket.

"For your appreciation, Monsieur!"

She put the basket on his knees, beside the lamb. It was full of green pods: small peas.

"Thank you, Madame," said the man. And he smiled pleasantly, while his hand rummaged among the pods.

But the lamb seemed even more excited than its master. It got up, bleating, and plunged its muzzle into the basket.

"Wait, Pascalot! They're for me, too," the old man complained, softly.

He took a handful of green pods and offered them to his pet. Then he bit into a few himself.

"Dare I offer you some, Mesdames?"

"No, no thank you!"

"You've doubtless lost the taste for natural aliments, and you only appreciate peas when they've been scalded with hot water and rolled in malodorous butter. My lamb and I have less depraved tastes, thank God, and we're as healthy as can be. Every afternoon we have a delicious meal like this, which earns us light digestion and pure dreams."

So saying, the man continued masticating his raw peas, contentedly.

The governess was nauseated. But Eve, being courageous, did not flinch. Such spectacles were not offered to her every day. The savage man, the ape-man—who claimed, then, that the type had disappeared? The anthropologists did not know where it was necessary to look.

Doubtless sated, the lamb leapt lightly to the ground, went to sniff a corner of the terrace, turned round, and honored the cement with a few dark pellets.

The two visitors no longer hesitated. Immediately, they rose to their feet. What were they going to see next?

But the peasant woman came back, companied by an old lady in somber attire.

"Oh, dear master, how happy I am!" the lady said, approaching the old man. "You've hurt your eyes, it seems? The newspapers informed us. Perhaps you don't recognize me? Comtesse d'Erbelick."

"Oh, my dear Madame! And how is Her Majesty?"

"Very well. She's downstairs, dear master. She sent me up to you. Can you receive her?"

"Of course! Ask Her Majesty to come up!"

"I will, dear master."

Eve and her governess looked at one another. What did it mean? A Comtesse? A Majesty, in the home of an eater of raw peas? Was it a joke?

"Will you excuse me, Mesdames," the old man said to them. "I have difficulty walking some days, and there are no electric bells here. Please will you ask for two more chairs to be sent up from the kitchen for Her Majesty the Queen of Bessarabia and her maid of honor."

"Oh, Monsieur!" exclaimed Eve, bowled over, "but we're leaving ourselves. It's already been such a long time...*au revoir*, Monsieur!"

"*Au revoir*, Mesdames!"

And, on the stairway with the creaking steps, Eve did indeed recognize Her Majesty Christia, Queen of Bessarabia, from the portrait that had appeared in several newspapers.

Petrified, she stopped, stood aside and bowed.

"Duck your head because of the beam," said the peasant woman.

"Oh, I know!" the Queen replied. "I've been here before, last year."

And a few seconds later, Eve heard the august voice uttering greetings, on the terrace, with a little explosion of joy: "Bonjour, dear friend! How well you look! I'm glad to see you. Let me kiss you!"

Eve went down, open-mouthed with amazement.

III. A Green and Gold Autograph

That evening, in the manor house on the outskirts of Bayonne where she was dining, Eve perceived a journalist. She did not know him very well, but when she left the table she went to offer him a cup of coffee, sugar and her most fulgurant smile.

Having drawn the man into a corner of the drawing-room, she said to him: "Monsieur, you must know the majority of the notable people in our neighborhood. Your newspaper publishes their names."

"Indeed, Mademoiselle."

"Can you tell me that of an old man who lives on the road to Saint-Jean-de-Luz, not far from Arbonne, on a farm called Larbouset?"

"Larbouset? I don't know it."

"A Basque house, rather banal, on a hill."

"There are quite a few Basque houses in that area, and quite a few hills. But what does your old man look like?"

"Tall, thin, with an enormous beard, almost entirely white.

"And he's a notable foreigner, you say?"

"So notable that the Queen of Bessarabia goes to see him, and calls him 'dear master' and 'dear friend.' I believe he's a doctor.

"A doctor. Do you mean Adrian?"

"I don't know. What does your Adrian do? Is he famous?"

"Very! A philosopher, an occultist, the author of resounding works, much discussed, on psychic forces and the mysteries of the Afterlife."

"Do you know the titles?"

"Yes, of course: *The Great Torment, Beneath the Veil of Isis*, etc. His last book, *Are they Really Dead?* has gone through forty of fifty printings. I believe, in fact, that he wrote it in Bayonne, or nearby, in the home of Basque peasants. He comes here every year, since the war. But he's not seen at the Café Farnier or Biarritz Casino. He has a horror of society."

"That must be him. Thank you, Monsieur."

"It might well be," the journalist continued, "that the Queen of Bessarabia goes to see him. She's lost a son, you know. And many inconsolable mothers come to find Adrian, or write to him. Anyway, he must have his portrait in Larousse, and it would be easy for you...there's surely a Larousse in the house? Let's look in there."

The journalist went into the nearby library, where there were a few smokers. Eve followed him in. They found the large volumes of Larousse easily. They opened the first and riffled through the letter A..."

"It's him! It' really him!" said Eve, with a small quiver of emotion. She saw an energetic face with a log white beard, and long hair, receding slightly. "It's him, but younger, of course. What does it say about him?"

Beside the portrait she read:

ADRIAN (Dr. Paul), spiritualist philosopher, author of The Great Inspired, Beneath the Veils of Isis, The Great Torment, The Impending Light, *etc. Born in Paris 1871, made his early studies...*

"My God!" remarked Eve. "He's only fifty-one..."
"Indeed. And you called him an old man."

"Why did I think so? That beard, no doubt. It ages him so much..."

"A fine handsome face, eh?" the journalist declared.

"Yes, very handsome," Eve admitted.

And she said that sincerely. How judgments were modified in accordance with circumstances! What is an ugly man, for a woman? Can a famous man be ugly?

"Oh, I've spoiled it a little, that face!" confessed Eve Illiberi, in a slightly vainglorious tone. "Can you imagine that I blacked his eye the other evening by throwing an apple? I've almost blinded him."

"Like amour? My compliments, Mademoiselle."

But Eve was no longer listening to the journalist.

Until the end of the soirée, she seemed distracted.

Having returned home to La Floride, her summer residence—for she lived in Bayonne, Bordeaux or even Paris during the winter—she went to consult the catalogue of her papa's books; but there was nothing by Adrian. Papa only bought works by members of the Institut, or novels crowned by the Académies, whose quality was guaranteed on the cover.

Adrian was doubtless not in any Académie. What a pity!

In bed, Eve racked her brains. *The Great Torment, Beneath the Veil of Isis, The Impending Light*...no, she had certainly not read any of those books, but it seemed to her that she had seen those titles in shop windows.

Well, she would go to procure them, immediately.

The next day, therefore, she went to Bayonne to buy them. She only found two: *The Great Torment* and *Are They Really Dead?*

On the way back in the auto she did not look at the mountains or the meadows; she did nothing but read.

How impassioning it was! Perhaps she did not understand very much of it, but what good are books whose depths and utmost depths one can fathom on the first reading? One might as well read a recipe book.

And that same day, she departed on foot for the great man's house. Yes, on foot and in a little olive-green outfit. The Queen had come in black with a fruit-seller's hat. Anyway, it was only two kilometers at the most: a stroll.

She left on her own without her governess. She was carrying the two volumes. It was a matter of obtaining an autograph. Provided that he could write! Oh, she was beginning to repent of having thrown that apple.

"Dr. Adrian?" she asked the peasant woman, at about six o'clock.

She had the joy of hearing the response: "In the garden, Mademoiselle. He's in the garden. Go straight ahead. The gate's open."

She was radiant. It was really him. *Him.*

"How is he?" she asked the peasant woman.

"A little better. His eye is no longer swollen."

"You're sure that I won't be disturbing him?"

"In fact...he sent away two people this morning. Will you remind me of your name?"

"Mademoiselle Illiberi. I've come before."

"I know. Will you wait here a moment."

Eve repented. *I had to...instead of going straight though...as long as he'll receive me now!*

She had an inspiration. "Wait, Madame! Take him these two books, and tell him that I'd like, with respect to certain pages...there's a chapter that I fear that I haven't understood..."

She started to blush like a little girl. What if she were sent away? Having put her hand on a great man, a

122

true one, whom Queens kissed, not to be able to obtain anything from him, not even two lines of handwriting!

But she breathed again. "Would you like to come, Mademoiselle? I really don't think you'll be disturbing him. He's at the far end of the garden, near the cabbage patch."

Eve launched forward, winged like Victory.

She found her great man between cabbages and broad beans, in the process of feeding his lamb in a grassy pathway. He was sitting on the trunk of a felled tree. He was holding a string at the end of which the lamb was capering. The same russet overcoat as the day before; a brown beret on this head—but on his feet, instead of slippers, he had clogs.

No bandage over his eyes; only violet bruises around one of them attested to the seriousness of the injury.

Eve appeared impressed. "Oh, Master! I see now. I see all the blackness of what I did. I want to get down on my knees again..."

"Don't do that," he said, very calmly. "You'll spoil your lovely dress on the damp grass...or your stockings, at least," he added, observing the brevity of the skirt.

Eve understood the justice of that reproach. Besides which, the Queen's skirt, the day before, had been long. The fashion was about to change.

"Are you still angry with me, Master? But chance alone is guilty. Why didn't my apple fall a second earlier, or a second later? Five centimeters to the left or the right? Oh, what rotten luck!"

"There is no chance, Mademoiselle. We call by that name something we don't understand. It's probable that your apple, obedient to mysterious impulsions, after a well-planned combination of circumstances, had to enter my eye on a particular evening in 1921, just as the crusaders entered Constantinople on a particular day in 1203. Neither of those events has any kind of importance, in any case."

"Oh!" protested the young woman. "No importance, an injury to the eye of a master like you? A philosopher, a thinker..."

Adrian's head turned toward the pretty girl. Lightning ought to be passing through that beard. The eyes, metallically cold, looked again at the silk stockings, the high heels, the low neckline, the rouged mouth and the white-powdered cheeks.

There was a terrible silence. Then the old man asked: "When will fashion permit young women to show their ears again?"

It was stinging. Eve understood the lesson. The thinker was telling her to observe distances. *Ne sutor ultra crepidam*, another had said.[7]

Let her talk about fabrics or the theater! What right did she have to dare to introduce herself to philosophy?

Eve could have wept.

"I know, Master, that my presumption would be enormous if I dared to raise with you the great problems around which your thought agitates. So I won't say any more about those things. Let me simply say to you that I'm glad to see that you're better, to see that your eye is healing and that you'll soon be able to get back to reading and writing. If you ever need me for anything whatsoever, even if it's only to procure you a book or a newspaper, go to a supplier, comb your lamb's

---

[7] "Shoemaker, don't go beyond to the shoe" (Pliny)—used colloquially to advise people to confine themselves to their own field of expertise.

fleece...I'm at your service—please feel free. When I arrived I had a foolish ambition—to ask you to put your signature on these two books of yours...but I no longer dare. *Bonsoir*, Master."

She had picked up her books. She curtsied, awkwardly, fearful of extending her hand...

It was charming, that hand: white, slender, perfect. And Nature rarely forgets her mission, which is to tender all sorts of pitfalls around two individuals she judges capable of being of use to one another. That hand had to be a redoubtable trap!

"You're delightful," said the old man. "Give me those volumes. You'd like an autograph?"

"Oh, Mater, if you would be so kind..."

"One ought to have every kindness for you. Come on, sit down here, beside me, on this fallen pear tree, which has no need of a furniture-maker to plane it to make an excellent seat. And tell me, I beg you, who are you, Mademoiselle?

"But..."

"I can see, as far as my ailing eyes permit me to, the color of your physical person, but I can see nothing of your moral person...and that's the only thing that counts, for me. Is your soul blonde or brunette? Is your heart rich or ruined? Only ruined hearts address themselves to men of my species, and I believe that yours has not yet encountered the slightest misfortune?"

"One never knows," murmured Eve, blinking nervously under those strange questions."

"Have you suffered, Mademoiselle?"

"Who hasn't suffered?"

"Have you suffered the pain that drives people insane, and makes them blaspheme and wish for death?

Have you lost someone very dear during the war? An only brother, an unforgettable fiancé?"

"I've never been engaged, Master."

"Well, it's scarcely any but those—the women who have lost an ardently beloved fiancé, husband, or son—with whom I can converse appropriately. If ever—and may you be spared such misfortune!—a frightful grief crushes you, remember me, and perhaps I'll be able to say consoling things to you."

"Oh, Master, you give me the desire to be unhappy, in order to have the right to be consoled by you."

"Thank you. You have generous impulses. Your soul must be blonde too. And I think that so many social miseries must be crushing you..."

"What miseries?" asked Eve, surprised.

"Your worldly duties: receptions, balls, theaters, dresses, sports, fashions...all the ligatures around the soul that prevent it from spreading and opening its wings. But for that, you'd probably be a delightful person, capable of thinking, of belonging to yourself, instead of belonging everyone—to yourself alone, or to some chosen friend—and I think they might take you very high, your wings."

"But I'd like nothing better than to open them, dear Master."

"What's the point?" sighed the doctor, closing his eyes.

And with a tender hand, he smoothed the fleece of his lamb, which had fallen asleep on him, like a child.

There was a silence of a few seconds. *An angel's passing over*, Eve would have said, in a drawing room. But she said nothing in that garden, so calm. She was thinking about wings.

126

Adrian opened his eyes again and discovered the two volumes between them.

"Hand me those books," he said, softly. "So you'd like an autograph?"

"Oh, if you'd deign..."

"I don't believe that I can write today; my injured eye can hardly see anything, and the other hasn't been able to see very much for two or three years."

"But it's necessary to have them treated!"

"What's the point? I can see sufficiently the spectacles that the future has in store for me. Then again, I have nothing on me with which to write. In any case, what significance can a drop of ink have, conventionally spread on a piece of paper? It's black, it's ugly, it's banal... Here's my autograph, Mademoiselle."

He picked a buttercup from the grass, slid it into one of the volumes between the fly-leaf and the title-page, and then closed the book and pressed it with both hands.

"There! It's a green and gold autograph. And you can read into it anything your imagination proposes: the homage of the summer, the memory of a dying flower, the tender confession of my garden..."

Eve looked at the crushed buttercup. On the white sheet, the corolla had imprinted a round patch the color of the sun.

"Thank you!" she said, kissing his head. And, obedient to some mysterious reflex, she kissed the skeleton of the flower.

After wards, she went away, very quickly, without saying anything, through the solitary garden, while the lamb, woken up by that abrupt departure, uttered an emotional bleat, as if to call her back.

IV. The Friend of Queens

Since, according to the words of the philosopher Adrian, nothing is due to chance, and the fall of an apple into the eye of a passer-by is determined, in the same way as the entry into Constantinople of the Crusaders, by an ensemble of logical and rigorous facts, what, then, on that last evening in June, obliged Eve to forget a volume in the garden of Larbouset, near the tree on which she had been sitting?

A laudable forgetfulness, undoubtedly, since it would give her the opportunity to go back.

But would she not have gone back anyway?

That man attracted her in an inexplicable manner.

To begin with, she had thought him repulsive; she was beginning to find him sympathetic. He was molded from a rare substance, and who can resist the seduction of the rare? He seemed to live differently from others, to act with less banality, to think more broadly and more highly. Anyway, for a Queen to have noticed him...

In her entourage, Eve had never heard words similar to the doctor's. The provinces are only interested in their crops and markets. Superior minds there go as far as discussing the future of aeronautics; never a frisson of poetry or art.

In the somewhat specialized society in which Eve moved, of joyful parvenus and intrepid speculators, people only talked about social receptions, coups on the Bourse, sport or politics. It was not admitted that a man, however small his fortune, should abstain from belonging to a club, going to bullfights and rolling around frenetically in a limousine with a prestigious brand-name.

128

Almost all notable people measured their glory by the dust they raised up on the roads.

And here was a famous man, visited by the greatest, who led a very narrow existence. He did not go to drink tea in a chic patisserie; he was ignorant of chic attire. He did not attribute any importance to the exterior life. All his luxuries were cerebral. He was less concerned with appearing than with effacing himself. And young Eve was no longer certain that that was madness.

She therefore went back to Larbouset, and all alone, like the last time, for her governess did not think there was the slightest danger in leaving her in the company of a man of that sort.

And they were hours of strong savor that she began to live in that hermitage, between the philosopher and his sheep.

She liked to persuade herself, in the early days, that a sentiment of Christian charity was guiding her; having done the man harm, did she not owe him assistance? But she soon recognized her error. The black eye had nothing to do with it. She came, not out of duty, but for pleasure. It was pleasant for her to breathe in the atmosphere of the scholar, to listen to him, to look at him. She no longer found him as old. When he smiled, a little of his youth reappeared in him, like the flutter of a wing lifting a lid. And one divined, beneath the lid, a sort of savage soul, a heart almost new.

He was not only young, he was handsome. The journalist had been right. That great beard did not do the philosopher any harm. And my God, one could wear round cuffs without being a monster.

She also appreciated Adrian's tall stature, his mat complexion, his slender nose, his sinuous and shapely mouth. As for his eyes—which became limpid again and lost their violet swellings—Eve found a strange light therein. Had she ever seen any so impressive? Two eyes of an exceedingly bright yellow, two open doors of a furnace. It was difficult to sustain the glare of those eyes, and it was astonishing not to see the eyelids crackling.

Only one thing could be criticized in Adrian's physique: his thinness. South of the Garonne, plumpness is not a vain word, and the idea that reigns in the stables is not yet banished from drawing-rooms. Undoubtedly, Parisian slimness is beginning to seduce southerners, but it is a fashion that will long meet with resistance.

Dr. Adrian was truly too emaciated. One could only admire a person of that style in the porch of a Roman church. Eve, who was rather replete, did not despair of extracting the philosopher from the vegetarian diet, the sole evident cause of that macabre wastage.

Almost every day, therefore, even when it rained, she arrived, via the coastal road that sometimes overhung the sea, sometimes plunged into pastureland, and showed a Pyrenean blue shoulder. She no longer wore elegant garments. She sought out outmoded costumes because the skirts were longer and the necklines higher, for she divined that if the doctor had welcomed her so poorly at first it was because of current fashions, so indecent. He was not one of those men that a beautiful leg hypnotizes and a prosperous cleavage excites with its cadences. All pitching made him seasick.

It was often up above, on the bright terrace, or down below, in his garden of beans and cabbages, that Eve found the Master, for he no longer went out much since the injury to his eye, being almost incapable of guiding himself. One afternoon, when he tried to come down toward her, he stumbled on the dark staircase. Then Eve permitted herself to offer him her arm, for the last few steps, and he accepted gladly. Since then, she had played the role of Antigone to that Oedipus.

It was, therefore, Eve who guided him in the garden, on the road, and even across fields. He liked the exercise; he had to walk for one or two hours a day in order that his legs would not get rusty. He had rheumatisms in his motor apparatus. He was always warm in the upper part of his body and cold in the lower part, his head in the sun and his feet in the ice: hence the traveling blanket over his knees, and even the woolly animal.

Eve had often strolled like that on the arm of a man. And almost always, whether the man was young or old, she had sensed a kind of insinuating weight of more-or-less discreet investigation in the direction of her rich bosom. Nothing similar in the arm of the dear Master. The man leaned no more tenderly on her than on a walking-stick. And that was not very flattering.

She went, nevertheless, proud of strolling on the arm of a famous man. Had he ever strolled on the arm of the Queen?

Thus, from time to time, Eve, the ex-socialite, had those frivolous surges of snobbery, But she hoped to get rid of them before long.

Sometimes, Adrian deigned to ask her: "Can you see the sea? Is it beautiful today? And what color are the mountains? Are they playing with their clouds like blue-clad little girls with their fluttering scarves?"

And, meekly, Eve told him the color of the sea and the mountains, and identified the rose-bushes that dangled over walls, their roses as curious as the faces of cheerful infants, and described the form of a parasol pine that seemed to be folding itself up in the distance under its round umbrella, in order better to hear the crickets.

And how beautiful the landscape must have seemed through the voice of that young woman!

Meanwhile, Eve learned things during those strolls, for Adrian sometimes deigned to make her confidences. He told her, for example, that if he was a vegetarian, it was not so much to obey the injunctions of his stomach as those of his heart. He loved animals so much. He did not understand how an honest man could kill them, or make them suffer. And he showed her that his garments were not made of wool but of cotton or vegetable fibers, how he warmed himself, not by means of leather but wood or hardened cardboard. And he added:

"An ordinary man who nourishes himself on meat causes, per year, the death of one ox, one pig, one or two sheep, and how much poultry? That represents an enormous quantity of murders, with which he loads his conscience in this world, and might perhaps earn him a frightful existence in the other. And to think that there are butchers, pork-butchers and hunters! Hell awaits all those bandits, if it exists. And if it doesn't exist, I shall ask the Master of All, loudly, to create one for them. When I suspect the existence of a worm in a fruit, I don't touch the fruit, and it's not out of disgust, but out of sympathy for the worm. Not to disturb the first occupant—that's the basis of all societies."

Eve listened respectfully to those strange words, which still seemed paradoxical to her, but whose profound meaning she might perhaps comprehend one day.

And Adrian also said to her:

"Why am I installed in this hovel of Larbouset? Because the view is very beautiful, very vast, the vastest in the region, and it's necessary to live in the heights to leave high works. There's a mountain in all great man, and even every God. Plato had Hymettus, Moses Sinai,

Jesus Tabor, Mahomet Hira. I have only Larbouset, because I have a sense of proportion. But if I thought I had genius, I'd install myself on Mont Blanc There's only a poor house here, devoid of comforts and conveniences, nothing that makes the joy of human beings, but the joy of the eyes is the sweetest of all, after that of the brain."

"And that of the heart?" Eve hazarded.

He looked at her severely. "I don't admit that there's any such viscera in me, Mademoiselle. I like to think that one day, human beings will no longer have a heart in the breast. If there is an evolution, it will be in that direction."

And, perhaps, unwittingly, her arm leaned a little more heavily on the doctor's. But the latter did not yield to that gentle pressure.

And another day, he said:

"Why do I have that lamb? Because I like lambs, because they're the symbol of tenderness, of purity. Besides which, you can see that they're so attached, as faithful as dogs. And how much more moving their voice is! It seems to me that a man who can hear a lamb bleat from time to time would never become malevolent. It must be for that reason that pastoral mores are so mild. Oh, my dear Pascalot! Go on, bleat! The world needs to hear you. I called him Pascalot, Mademoiselle, because I saved his life one Easter day. I saw him passing along the road in a cart. He was going to be sold to a butcher. He was so meek! We loved one another right away. Another thunderbolt for an animal! I'm attached to so many animals!"

"Only to animals?" Eve risked, in a low voice, looking at the ground.

Adrian did not reply. He picked a hawthorn flower from a hedge and sniffed it slowly.

"Oh, you've pricked yourself, Master! Your hand is bleeding..."

"Naturally. That flower couldn't embalm me without doing me harm. It's in the natural order. And I'll soon be bleeding too, because of that lamb, from which it will be necessary to separate myself. One ought never to do good. It's so good that one is obliged to suffer for it."

"But why will it be necessary for you to separate from it?"

"Because it will become wicked, because it will be at the terrible age of amour... Oh, amour, what a calamity!"

With that the silence recommenced and the young woman no longer dared trouble it. Why was Adrian so bitter when he pronounced the word *amour*? She suspected that the philosopher had suffered a great deal. Perhaps some Queen?

She was still embarrassed by those long silences. In society they would have appeared very inconvenient. The racket of conversation always had to fly there, even when one had nothing to day. Eve could not get used to these new habits. One day, Adrian understood that his mutism might be poorly interpreted. Then he showed her to men in a nearby field who were laboring side by side, bent over, in silence.

"They're two brothers," he told Eve. I know them. They're together morning and evening, and they never tell one another anything."

"Perhaps they detest one another?"

"They adore one another."

Eve blushed. How good those words sounded to her! "They adore one another..." She lowered her head, smiling, and continued walking, in silence, between the man and the lamb.

When they did not go for a walk the doctor accepted, without displeasure, that the young woman read aloud to him a page from a review, and that she open his letters. With what joy she would have become his secretary!

I've injured your eyes take mine! she had wanted to say to him. *And take my arms if yours are fatigued. Take...*

What would she not have permitted him to take? She experienced, at his approach, all the confidence, all the docility that superior beings impose. For she had to judge him superior rather than mad. But how many follies compose a superiority?

Every day she appreciated more the singularities of the man, which had once seemed so shocking to her. He made extremely disrespectful judgments of the rich, whom he detested, sports, which he scorned, and industrial science, which he feared, accusing it of gradually preparing the end of the world, and he had such a force of persuasion in saying those enormities that Eve felt troubled, disorientated, and perhaps convinced.

She was like a child to whom someone has said: "Admire this, respect that, desire these magnificent things, hoist yourself toward these summits," and to whom, suddenly someone who passes for a sage, whose value is proclaimed by the world great men comes to cry, on the contrary: "Close your eyes! All that appeared beautiful to you is ugly! The only magnificence is within you!" How loudly Adrian seemed to speak to her! She was always astonished not to see him on a mountain. And when he fell silent, he ought to have been higher still: in the clouds.

She became sad, however, in the evenings, as soon as she found herself alone again, in her room at La Floride. How distant that man was from her! The lamb she had tamed, for it sometimes came to go to sleep on a flap of her dress. But Adrian seemed to be afraid of her dress. Never, doubtless, could she inspire tenderness in a man so master of himself, who froze at the first allusion to amour. And Eve's twenty years revolted.

If, at least, he had deigned to open, not his heart, since he professed not to have one, but his brain! He also remained refractory in that direction. He never talked about his works, or his projects. He did not admit that she had curiosities about theosophy, about the afterlife, about the invisible world that interested him so profoundly. She had seen clearly, in reading *Beneath the Veil of Isis*, that he devoted himself to occult sciences, that he carried out experiments in telepathy, levitation, not to mention spiritualism. But when she broached those terrible problems before him, he went back into his tower and seemed once again to be clamoring: *Ne sudor*...

However, he always permitted her to come back, to give him her arm for a walk, and to read to him on rainy days. It is true that his eyes, he said, were still so poorly, so weak...

Would he ever be healed?

One day, she arrived two hours earlier than usual. She went upstairs without warning. And what did she see, after having penetrated into the bedroom? The master at his work-table. He was writing.

"Oh, what joy! You're cured!" she said.

Adrian seemed very troubled. He threw down his pen-holder with a sort of ill-humor and began blushing like a child.

"Cured! You can write, finally! And very well, it seems to me" And very fine handwriting! How happy I am!"

But she dared not continue. Adrian's cheeks were crimson. His eyes were moist. He seemed utterly ashamed of having been surprised in the act of writing. Oh, why?

The lamb came to rub against Eve's dress. She caressed its neck. Adrian's hand was also posed on that neck. And Eve's hand was so close that she could feel its warmth.

Were they not going to join together, those two hands, between which all the electricity in the world seemed to be quivering?

But Adrian stood up, without saying another, and went on to the terrace. He did not stumble. He was walking with a firm step.

Then Eve blushed in her turn, believing that she understood. She put her hands on her bosom to help her contain all her joy.

Monsieur Adrian could see, then? For how long? His eyes could not have opened to the light in a single night, like the buttercups in his garden.

He was pretending. Oh, why? To have his arm on the arm of the young woman? To have the eyes of the young woman close to his own? What a discovery!

Eve headed for the terrace. But now it was she who was stumbling, unsteadily.

"Master!" she said, going toward him, her hands joined.

He turned toward her; and his eyes appeared to be full of tears.

"No, I beg you!" he said. "Leave me! Go away! And don't come back any more, if you please!"

"Oh!"

"Don't come back any more, if you love me a little."

They looked at one another for a second. Then their heads bowed, almost simultaneously.

Eve went away.

Adrian caressed his lamb.

The parasol pine in the distance seemed to be reaching up into the light, as if it could see, in the depths of the sky, something marvelous.

V. At the Feet of the Tyrant

"If you love me a little," he had said!

He knew, then?

And now, she knew too.

She was beloved, and perhaps more than a little. That trouble, those tears, the sound of his voice, so sad. She was beloved.

Oh, how that thought did her good! It filled her brain with sunlight, gave her the impression of being entirely gilded, all ripe, like a cluster of grapes that would like to dissolve under the feet of a wine-trader.

And yet, he had forbidden her to go back!

What had amour done to him, then, to inspire such dread?

Eve obeyed. She did not go up the hill to Larbouset again. She tried to return to the former plane, to the former horizons.

Poor horizons! Adrian's shadow striped them all.

Eve consulted the cards recently received, which invited her to social celebrations or intimate meetings. She showed herself again in a few drawing rooms in Biarritz and Saint-Jean-de-Luz. But who had shrunk the people there, taken the varnish off the furniture and the color out of everything? She no longer found the women beautiful or the men witty.

And what did they talk about? Madame Haramboure's new necklace! She remembered that Adrian had said to her one evening: "A pearl is a gross counterfeit of nacre. Let us admire the humility of the woman who finds her happiness in that which the torment of an oyster makes."

Did they talk about the prowess of a Parisian boxer who was going to be the next world champion? She remembered this reflection by Adrian: "I'd like to see him at odds with that ox grazing over there. When will the biography of the ox be in the newspapers?"

Did they make speeches about some scientific discovery? She thought of what Adrian had said to her on another day: "Science, or at least what is called by that name in the industrial world, is the sickness of the planets. When the Great Master judges that a planet is blameworthy he inflicts the scientific microbe upon it, thanks to which people exterminate one another thereon while awaiting the supreme Scientist, the Genius of Destruction, and Antichrist of Annihilation, who will pulverize it by means of one of those marvelous scientific discoveries of which we are so proud. 'Make way for others!' The Great Master will say, sweeping away the detritus. And we will certainly have deserved it."

One day, at a garden party, Eve encountered an American millionaire about whom everyone at Biarritz was talking. She recalled that when she was on Adrian's arm once she had seen that sensational man's automobile go past. And what had the Master said about him? "Poor slave! His millions take him everywhere he pleases. He's obliged to obey all the fashions. 'Come here,' orders one. 'Run there,' orders another. And there are those that howl: 'Dress like this! See people like these! Eat dishes like these! Love women like these! Do these things! Don't do those any longer!' Oh, the roaming beggar! He's free to go ask for his bread at any door he pleases, to go to sleep under any fern that tempts him. Introduce me to that beggar, if you have the honor of knowing him."

It was evidently excessive, but how flavorsome! Those bold paradoxes, Adrian launched with such authority that they took on the appearance in his mouth of elementary truths.

Another time, Eve found in society a famous factory owner who was reputed to have three thousand workers and first class tools. And what had been the Master's sentiment regarding that man?

"He's an unconscious evildoer. He's preparing the universal Revolution that will bloody the world. Mechanization causes laborers to lose the taste for their labor. And what will the laborers do when they no longer want to labor? Once, an artisan prepared, fabricated and fitted all the pieces of an apparatus himself. He saw his work born, he watched it grow. He loved it. Nowadays, there are factories where a worker only makes one bolt. Al his life he will make the same bolt. And inevitably, he will detest the work that mechanization renders monotonous, tedious and absurd.

"Brutalized by his work, he will seek distractions in the tavern, among prostitutes, in all the places where one slides into drunkenness, strikes and revolt. The more machines are made, the more revolutionaries are made. The true men of progress do not concern themselves with what can be extracted from metals, gases and retorts, but with what can be extracted from hearts. There alone is the divine matter that ought to make us advance toward perfection."

Eve could no longer spend an hour in her frivolous society of bankers, snobs and idlers without the silhouette of Adrian looming up, tall and severe, between herself and others. In a matter of days the man had erased in the depths of her what several years of education had inscribed there. Did spell-casters and sorcerers still exist, then?

Even André de X****, about whose eyes all the young women were crazy, and Gaston I***, whose intelligence all the mothers praised, appeared to her to be dull and ridiculous. Amour takes all the light scattered in the universe and projects it in a powerful beam on a single person. It is futile to search for a stray ray; there is only darkness.

She thought: *Am I going to be stuck in this absurd sentiment? Can I, the socialite, the elegant, fêted young woman with my court of young suitors, really be in love with a sort of old savage? Where would that take me? To a banal adventure of the flesh? I wouldn't want that. To a commerce of minds? He's the one who refuses it. I believe that I've just strayed into a blind alley. Oh, to be able to turn back...!*

She tried, but in vain. She tried wearying herself by day: dancing, flirting, frolicking with young friends in the evenings; by night, she dreamed of the Great Friend, of the Only Friend. As soon as her limbs stopped, her brain took its revenge. One thinks that one is master of oneself, but one perceives, in one's depths, a usurper that is governing. And people dream of ruling the world!

Several days went by; Eve did not forget Adrian.

And him—did he forget Eve? How she would have liked to know.

One afternoon, she dared to walk toward Larbouset. At a slow pace, she followed the coast road that shows a corner of blue sea here, and the rump of a bluer mountain there. But those various azures did not interest her. She only looked at the passers-by on the road. None of them showed her the skeletal and bearded form of Adrian.

Two hundred meters from Larbouset, Eve heard a plaintive bleating. Oh! The lamb! Pascalot! It had to be him!

Eve's heart leapt. It really was the lamb. How tender its voice sounded! Wasn't it calling her? Hadn't it divined that its old friend was nearby? These young animals have so much flair.

For five minutes Eve remained indecisive.

Shall I go there? she wondered. *What will he say if I suddenly go into his room, in spite of his prohibition? Will he have the strength to scold me? Doesn't he think about me a little, since I think about him so much?*

The lamb continued to bleat, to lament.

Come on! You'll be happy. We'll all be happy, its plaintive voice signified...

Eve turned round. No, she didn't dare. She turned round, her head bowed, on the burning road, where brief flurries of wind, perhaps precursors of a storm, were picking up the dust here and there and sending it toward the clouds, in smoky spirals, as if the earth were catching fire.

She turned back, sad to the point of tears, toward her crushing La Floride. Why did the wind not sweep through her as it did over the road? Why did it not take away her heart, her wretched and useless heart?

The lamb was no longer bleating. Nothing could be heard but a shrill cicada, and the undisciplined August wind that was crackling the trees, disturbing the tresses of the bushes, causing spasms in the heather, whistling in the thatch and across the shaven fields, as if in millions of short flutes.

Eve raised her arms in order to feel the wind in her moist armpits. The wind caresses us there on certain days, as if it were searching for our lost wings.

Abruptly, though, she shuddered. Oh! Her redis-covered wings....

Over there, near her home, facing the Saint John apple tree what overhung the road, a man was sitting on the bank: an old man with a gray beard and a russet overcoat....

Adrian. It could only be Adrian.

At that sight, Eve's eyes fluttered. Adrian! He had come toward her at the same time as she had gone to-ward him. What a coincidence! In their depths, therefore, was it the same tyrant who governed, who commanded? Oh, the kindness of that tyrant, master of the world!

Amour! She said to herself, paling with happiness. *Amour, it's really him. What does he want with us, then?*

She advanced lightly, unconsciously, carried away by the summer wind like the grains of sand on the road.

Adrian must not have seen her yet. He remained seated, imperturbably, on his bank. And his eyes, it seemed, were contemplating the apple tree facing him, the beautiful Saint John apple tree, whose nervous branches the wind was tormenting.

Why was he looking at it like that, the dear tree that had been the cause of their meeting? Had he a grudge against it? Was he thinking it?

From time to time he turned his head toward the nearby villa, whose red roof burst forth through the ver-dure. Perhaps he was hoping for something from that direction: to glimpse a familiar form, to hear a familiar voice?

But Eve arrived from the opposite direction, with-out making any noise. She was only fifty paces away.

Adrian perceived her.

Then he stood up, suddenly, and remained motion-less in the middle of the road like an inert block. Then he took his hat off, slowly, and took two steps toward Eve. His face was distraught. Was he suffering? Was he suffering? Very difficult to tell. It was nothing but a long frisson drawing nearer. In his eyes he had the confusion of children caught at fault.

"Oh! I didn't expect…," he tried to say.

"Me neither…," she stammered.

But they soon sensed, both of them, the poverty of that lie.

And their hands came together, pressed one another, held on to one another, as ivy enlaced an elm.

They took a few steps side by side, without saying anything, and their difficult breathing revealed a sudden oppression. One might imagine that high above, far from the earth, aviators sometimes breathe like that.

But the tyrant that was within them had pushed them toward the sea, toward the gate of the orchard—the gate through which, one evening, Eve had emerged from her enclosure, her legs bare and her hair in the wind, to ask forgiveness of the unknown man that an apple had wounded. On that gate Eve's right hand pushed, the left still remaining in Adrian's.

The gate opened. They went in together, into the long grass, where a few late daisies, slightly withered, were showing all the petals they lacked, as if the wind, in passing, had wanted to know whether it was loved a little, a lot, or passionately…

Adrian followed, fearful, without pronouncing a word. What would they have been able to say that they did not know?

Having arrived at the foot of the tree, however, Eve ventured: "I want to show you my apple tree. You know? The one that…" Then she dared to ask—so softly that a hairy bumble-bee hovering over a lupin was buzzing more loudly: "Do you still hold a grudge against it?"

Adrian closed his eyes and replied, in a low voice: "No."

"Thank you."

And, raising the Master's hand, she posed her lips upon it.

"Thank you," she repeated. "And thanks to him."

She leaned toward the trunk of the apple tree and, as she had kissed his hand, she kissed the bark.

Did the apple tree experience anything at the contact of her lips? It caused an apple to fall shortly thereafter. Five or six still remained up above, which the wind was jostling forcefully. Eve picked it up, hesitated for a second, and then offered it to her friend.

Then, there were many tears that appeared in the eyes of the old man.

"Eve," he murmured, "Listen to me. I have something to tell you, something very serious. For so many days, it's been tormenting me. Oh, I've understood how difficult it would be for me live far away from you. May I speak?"

"Please do."

"Where?"

"Under our apple tree."

"I'd like that."

"Come. Sit down there. Leave me your hand. I'm listening, friend."

VI. Under the Apple Tree

This is how Adrian spoke, sitting under the Saint John apple tree, in the deserted orchard, beside Eve, who listened to him, so emotional that she scarcely dared to interrupt him.

"Mademoiselle, I have no need to tell you that I have contracted for you, in a few days, the most tender of affections. And you understand that if I employ the word 'affection' it is because another word, so frequent on human lips, ought no longer to be pronounced by mine.

"You must be twenty years old; I'm fifty, and I shall not commit the impropriety of forgetting it. I believed that my heart was invulnerable, for it too has been plunged in the waters of the Styx, but I have felt keenly, at the sight of you, at your approach, that that heart was like Achilles' heel. The person who dipped it in the black river forgot to immunize the place where her fingers held it.

"You're pretty, Mademoiselle Eve, and all the seductions of the first Eve are within you, and I have had the displeasure of discovering that I still have some of the weaknesses of Adam. I am deeply ashamed of that.

"But I perceived that your affection could be sweet for me, and that, inspired by you, I might perhaps succeed in doing great things, in fulfilling a certain mission that I imposed on myself thirty years ago. I beg you, therefore, to grant me, if it is possible, your precious collaboration."

"Anything that pleases you, Mater," the young woman said, lowering her eyelids under Adrian's gaze—

a sharp gaze, which passed like two searchlights into the depths of her being.

"That collaboration, if I obtain it from you meekly, might perhaps have incalculable results for human beings. It's a matter of their happiness, their repose, their confidence in the future. It's matter, in brief, of appeasing the 'Great Torment' of which I've spoken in one of my books, which is the uncertainty we are in as to what awaits us after death.

"I don't know whether you have faith, Mademoiselle: a robust, well-reasoned, indestructible faith. Those who do are very happy. The Great Torment does not afflict them. They are convinced that in doing good on earth they will rediscover in the heavens the dear beings that they have lost. And they fulfill all their duties, accept all sacrifices. They are altruistic out of egotism, which is the result of all well-conceived religions.

"Unfortunately, the number of believers is diminishing every day. Scientists, philosophers, and rationalists are gnawing away at our religions like woodworm at a rotten beam. And the old edifice is in the process of cracking over society. One senses the impending disasters. There are distressed minds that would like to believe, but no longer can; which would like to think that everything is not finished when the body has been carried away between four planks, but who dare not. It is for those minds that I labor, that I seek, that I battle with the Mystery. And perhaps, if you support me in that struggle, I will succeed in penetrating it, the terrible Mystery.

"And what a victory it would be if, thanks to us, the Great Torment were attenuated somewhat! Oh, I don't have the pretention of abolishing it entirely, but if I could render it less acute, more tolerable! If you knew how many people are suffering!

"I receive confidences and letters on a daily basis. 'Console me!' people write to me from all parts of the world. 'Tell me that I will rediscover one day the person I have lost, that death has not destroyed him entirely, that he is still with me, close to me!'

"And don't think that I'm alone in receiving those lamentations.

"All those who have treated the Mystery in their books hear the innumerable plaints of people who are suffering and would like to be cured. And those people go to consult, not only theosophists, but spiritualists, chiromancers, Tarot-readers—the thousand charlatans who exploit the Afterlife. Those unfortunates are in all classes of society. Can they never be relieved?

"The official scientists of the last century have decreed that the soul is a secretion of the bran, the mind an emanation of matter, as the perfume is an emanation of the flower. And they have had the stupidity to affirm, in consequence, that the soul does not survive the brain, nor the perfume the flower.

"But can one not make this response? Take a rose, macerate it is a certain liquid and then distil that liquid in a certain fashion; what happens? The rose dies but the perfume does not. It persists, one can conserve it for ten years or a hundred years in a bottle. And who can tell whether the Earth, the Sun, the rain and the wind are not themselves, with regard to souls, what distillers are with regard to perfumes? Whether the spirits of the dead are not disengaged and conserved in unknown regions?

"And besides, since everyone needs to believe in survival, is not survival real? Can one admit that it is in vain that nature has rooted such a unanimous sentiment in humans? No. Nature does not deceive; she merely veils. One day, we shall see, when our eyes are worthy of the splendor.

"Oh, Mademoiselle Eve, do you sense all the good that we could do for human beings if we could make that veil fall immediately? How people would bless us! How glad we would be to have given such happiness! Do you feel it, tell me? And do you want it?"

He had taken her hands; he squeezed them, agitated them, and his eyes filled with an unknown radiance that seemed to come from another world.

He was transfigured. He was no longer fifty years old but thirty, twenty. Every passion is a rejuvenation. Whoever is devoted is embellished. Every noble thought becomes an adornment.

Eve admired him.

"Do I want it?" she replied. "Oh, yes, yes! But have I really merited it?"

"You will merit it. I've looked within you. At first I only discovered—shall I confess it to you—mundane poverties, but afterwards I believed that I discovered an admirable richness of sentiments that dazzled me.

"You must remember the repulsion I had in the early days about talking to you about my works, yielding to you my most cherished ideas. I defended my threshold. But today, I am opening it to you, charmed, and saying to you: 'Enter, young woman. All my old man's soul is yours.'"

"How I thank you for that! But it's very troubling. What do you expect of me? A collaboration, you say? What do you mean by that, Master? How can the ignorant girl that I am collaborate with the great scientist that you are?"

"By living near me, my mingling your days with mine, your thoughts with mine. Oh, don't be afraid! Our bodies will no longer exist. It's a marriage of minds that I want. You've sensed the horror that I have of what the world calls amour, which is nothing but the more-or-less unconscious attraction of two bodies. I had striven to strip away all flesh. However, you came, you who revealed yourself at first as a magnificent efflorescence of flesh...that Saint John's Eve, do you recall?...you came to persuade me that some still existed around me, that I was a man almost as weak as so many others...and I held it against you."

"Forgive me, Master! I must have been mad, that Saint John's Eve."

"You were a woman, you were an Eve going radiantly toward her objective, the doom of Adam; you were the unconscious and marvelous motor that bears away the world. Toward what? We have no idea. And you almost dragged me away in your splendid whirlwind. It was nearly twenty years since a similar weakness had overtaken me. For I had sworn never to linger before a woman, since a woman had done me so much harm, not only in my flesh but in my spirit. And perhaps I owe you an explanation of that statement.

"I was once married, Mademoiselle Eve. My wife was very beautiful. I adored her. I also wanted to make her my collaborator. We worked and we dreamed together. We undertook sessions in hypnotism, thought transmission, levitation, materialization...what do I know? After a few months, I believed that I had made conclusive experiments. Disincarnate spirits showed themselves to me: I photographed them, heard them, and palpated them. An extraordinary medium opened the portals of the Unknown to me. He was an Italian. Of all

151

that he revealed to me, I made a book. And what a book! The Mystery would be pierced through, the shadow definitely dissolved. Humankind would be precipitated toward the Light, arrive in the stars…it was conclusive. The most incredulous would proclaim their faith…

"As my book was about to be published, I received an anonymous letter. I watched my wife and perceived that she was deceiving me with my medium, that both of them were mocking me, that my finest experiments were tricks, that my deductions were false. What a discovery! I thought I would die of it.

"Hence my aversion for women, especially the prettiest, for they are often the most treacherous. Beauty is only the mask of Pain in search of prey. But you came, and I understood that there could also be beautiful and good women, charming and loyal, capable of interesting themselves in the work of an old man. And the collaborator that I thought I had found in my wife, it seemed to me that destiny was presenting to me in you. And a certain capital experiment, which I wanted to undertake with her, it seems to me, Mademoiselle Eve, that I might one day attempt with you."

"What experiment, Master?"

"Permit me to remain silent still. It's a grave matter. If I talked to you about it today, you'd probably suspect my reason. But in time, I hope that I'll be able to explain myself without passing for a lunatic in your eyes. Trust me, young friend. The time will come.

"In the meantime, I only ask permission to listen to you, to walk with you through the countryside, among the simples, as we have one for a few weeks. I confess that in asking you that, I'm obeying a vulgar instinct, so difficult to extirpate in our terrestrial clay. I want to go toward God resolutely, but as a little of the human still remains in me, I think that I will make the journey more agreeably beside a pretty woman like you. That is the simple explanation of my conduct. Accept, and you will render me very happy. Thus, little by little, we would establish between us such a harmony such a communion, that the great proof of which I have dreamed for such a long time could be attempted."

"But..."

"Don't interrogate me anymore. Be the first incurious Eve, the first serious Eve. Enough others are devoting themselves to the frivolities of this world. If my plan succeeds, you will only interest yourself in the problems of the other. You will be the Eve of the Re-elevation, as the first was the Eve of the Fall; you will guide man to Bliss, as the first led him to Sin. Oh, how we will love one another, after our death!

"Adieu. I've said too much. I've pronounced the divine word that so many human lips profane. I'm going. Adieu! *A bientôt!*"

"Until tomorrow, if you wish! I'll come to your house tomorrow."

"Well, yes—until tomorrow!"

"And forever."

"And forever. I want to believe that the future will not prove you wrong. Forever! And let me thank in my turn the unforgettable tree to which we owe our meeting, the Tree of Life and Death, the Tree of the New Science."

He surrounded the trunk of the apple tree with one of his arms, as one puts one's arm around the torso of a friend. Then he went away through the long grass, toward the nearby road, where the warm wind that continued to lift up the ocher dust seemed to be blowing mad kisses, in its own fashion, toward the clouds.

VII. A Philosopher Speaks

A new existence began for Eve, and how different it was from the old! Almost every day, she went to see Adrian at Larbouset. And as before, although he had recovered his sight and his legs had become firm again, he walked, in dreams, on her arm.

And now he talked; he found her worthy of listening to elevated verities, of pondering upon grave problems.

He commented on his books to her, revealed his projects to her, confided his most secret thoughts to her. Gradually, he drew her toward the superior plateaux where the timid feet of elegant women so rarely venture. She followed him there joyfully.

And, as she went higher, the low valleys in which she had frolicked previously disappeared in a mist

How could so many of her peers interest themselves in the form of new hats, read reports of social events, palpitate in following with their eyes a galloping horse or a man driving a balloon?

Bestialities, regressions, falls back into darkness of beings departed for the stars.

Her Master, her fine thinker whose eyes seemed two solar sources, permitted her to read the innumerable letters in which so many strangers confided their torment to him and asked him for consolation—and he asked her to reply to those unhappy individuals.

She became his secretary. Together, they leafed through scientific journals, took cognizance of new discoveries. Their brains fraternized, their minds caressed one another, like two amorous birds who, before uniting, brush one another with their wings. But Adrian never permitted himself any equivocal pressure on Eve's arm, nor any excessively tender smile toward the young lips that parted instinctively as if to welcome other lips.

No, undoubtedly, the shadow of carnal amour would never again weigh over them. They would only be two passionate souls, embracing in the light, on high, with the approval of the angels.

When the weather was fine, all three of them set forth—for the lamb Pascalot usually participated in the fêtes—and Adrian took Eve to some bare hill in the Basque country where gorse or ferns flourished. And there, in the silent desert, he talked to her about profound and puerile things, which bore no resemblance to the words being exchanged, at the same hour, on the fashionable beaches glimpsed down below, in a gilded haze.

He said to her: "Do you know, Eve, that we're living in a formidable epoch, in which the fate of humankind is being decided. All of the living have believed that their epoch was the most critical of all. That idea is very human. But I don't think that people have ever been obliged to live in a greater anguish. Their guides, for a hundred years, have been blindly driving them toward the abyss. Materialists, positivists, rationalists: those are the names of the dogs that are guiding the flock.

"And see what they have made of them: madmen, starvelings, gamblers who, expecting nothing after their death, steal from one another and kill one another in order to put as much enjoyment as possible into their existence. Since everything is finished afterwards, they want to extract everything beforehand. They precipitate themselves toward wealth, power and amour. Three-quarters of the living measure their merit by the number of millions they have accumulated, or women they have held in their arms, or bottles of champagne they have drunk, or rosettes of various colors that they have the right to sport on their lapels.

"Their ideal is beneath the one that haunted the prehistoric caverns. People do not eat everything raw, but they tear it apart with eager teeth. To do good is nothing but the gesture of imbeciles. To be virtuous dishonors. All crapulousness is praised, respected and deified. All terrestrial politics, among people of whatever color, can be defined by the formula: *Flatter the Beast*. So it rears up, the Beast; it stretches out its claws and shows its fangs. All government becomes impossible. The universal Revolution is beginning. 'Hate one another!' preach the new prophets. And one can wonder whether the Master of Everything, sickened by the spectacles that we offer him, has not resolved to purify the plant by means of a deluge of blood.

"Yes, young woman with golden hair, with splendid flesh and eyes as pure as two violets in the dew, Eve, harbinger of so many joys, you were born in an epoch promised to all dolors, and I believe that, save for a miracle, you will see frightful things.

"But the miracle might occur. I expect it. And it seems to me that its light is already over us. And that miracle will be a new religion, so strong, so pure, so evident that it will no longer find any atheists. That religion will be scientific, in the elevated sense of the word; it will impose itself like the light of day. It will make us better, since it will demonstrate mathematically that in being good to others we will be good for ourselves; since it will establish that we are in our present life what we have merited being in an anterior life, that we shall be tomorrow what our actions today will have made of us.

"The majority of religions allow us to believe all that, but they have not proven anything; they do not render those moral sentiments sensible, mechanically, as we demonstrate by a laboratory experiment that water is a compound of hydrogen and oxygen. The religion of which I dream, and which it is important to establish as soon as possible, will also be easily demonstrable. It will be no more mysterious that the functioning of a steam engine or the automatism of a child's toy. All of its inner workings will be visible, all of its benefits tangible.

"At this moment, my young friend, all over the world, thousands of scholars like me are in search of that magnificent and necessary religion. And one can believe that a few capital discoveries—like that of Hertzian waves, for example—will suffice for it to impose itself upon the world.

"Eve, I swear to you that. I'm not delirious, that I'm not having extravagant dreams. A new religion is in progress. It will regenerate humankind. The present terrors, disorders and troubles are indications of a prodigious birth. God will be reborn; the splendid God of which previous religions have only been the obscure masks. And I hope that we shall play some part in that birth. Yes, me, the old man, and you, the young woman. And the force that drove us toward one another will not have done so in vain...I hope! I hope! By virtue of our supernatural love, we will hasten the advent of the new God..."

"But how?" asked Eve, putting her hands together and making herself very humble next to the strange man who spoke to her in the tone of a prophet.

Then the old man fell silent, for he did doubtless not consider her sufficiently prepared.

And he closed his eyes again, as if to see the magnificence of the future more clearly.

At other times, sitting next to Eve under one of the large local chestnut-trees that writhe in the sea breeze but want to laugh regardless, showing the black teeth of their thorny fruits, Adrian suddenly placed one of his hands on the young woman's forehead, and said, in a commanding tone:

"Look at me! In the eyes! Again! Again!"

And, seeing her shiver under his gaze, her murmured: "Thank you. That's good. We'll succeed. You'll be an agent of the perfect liaison between the two worlds."

"Which worlds, Master?"

"This one and the one above. Few people, during their terrestrial life, can go from one to the other, but I believe that you might. And that's excellent for my enterprise. The world above is full of marvels. You'll show them to the one below."

And after a long silence, in which the furnaces of his eyes refreshed themselves in the spectacle of some gentian flower that had the appearance of a drop of azure fallen into the heather, he said to his friend:

"You see that hairy plant? Touch it. Good. With my microscope, I'll study the reaction. You're overflowing with life. You'll embellish thousands of other lives."

All that remained very obscure for Eve, such a novice....

But Adrian would not consent as yet to explain himself more clearly.

Another day, in his room at Larbouset, he showed her a bizarre apparatus that came from Paris. Under a glass bell-jar there was a metal needle suspended horizontally by a thin wire over a dial, laid flat and bordered by numbers like the face of a watch. It was called a biometer.[8]

Adam said to Eve: "Put your hand on that glass dome... Good. Stay there."

She observed that the needle turned at the end of its wire, under the bell-jar. She manifested some surprise.

"Is my hand doing that?" she asked.

"Yes, it's your hand."

"Through the glass? How can that be?"

"It can, as you see. Advance your left hand now. At the approach of your left hand, the needle begins to oscillate again, but in the opposite direction."

"Well!" exclaimed Eve, as an expression of bewilderment.

Adrian looked at the numbers. He seemed satisfied.

"That's very good," he declared. "Your fluid is remarkable. I believe we'll obtain excellent results."

"But can you tell me how, without touching the needle...?"

"You're moving it? No, I can't tell you. But can we explain everything around us? I'll show you even more remarkable things. Patience, young friend."

That same day, on the terrace of Larbouset, before the immense landscape, over which clouds were slowly parading their shadows like mobile dimples, Adrian said to Eve:

---

[8] In 1922, as today, the term biometer was conventionally used to describe devices for measuring carbon dioxide output from living bodies. The device given that name here is, however, one popularized by the French occult theorist Hippolyte Baraduc, notably in his book *L'Âme humaine* (1896; tr. as *The Human Soul*).

"The mistake of the majority of human beings is only to believe what they see. They ought, however, to begin to realize that our senses only reveal to us the millionth part of the things that exist. Our eyes, our fingers, our ears, our nostrils and out mucous membranes deceive us. Without the telescope, we would know nothing about the stars; without the microscope, we would know nothing about infusoria. The heavens appear to us to be empty, and it has been proven to us that there is nothing there but a void. We already know that there are billions of creatures in a drop of water; we shall know one day how many there are in a bubble of air. And what are those aerial beings? Do they not emanate from us?

"You doubtless think that your body finishes where your flesh finishes, but I've just shown you that your body extends much further than your fingernails, since one of your fingers can displace a copper needle several centimeters away, in spite of an intervening glass bell-jar. In any case, the mimosa, a plant that can be found in all hothouses, has shown you that already. Yes, my young friend, you act much further away than you think, not merely with the gestures of your fingers but with the thoughts of your brain. Around us there is still a presence, a presence that we feel but cannot see, a real presence that can already be photographed. Silver bromide, better endowed that the eye of a man of genius, is beginning to perceive various layers around us, fluid envelopes, auras of various colors—and all that is not faked, it seems.

"Some scholars claim that a person who is thinking emits innumerable waves, that an angry individual moves within a kind of tempest while a happy one floats in an azure halo. I'll show you books with very clear plates, which represent all that. I say it to you again,

160

Eve: the science of the materialists will bring us back to spiritual science. The atheists are in the process of revealing God to us. From discovery to discovery, step by step, we are climbing toward Hm. One more effort, and perhaps we shall see him face to face."

"But that makes one tremble!"

"Yes I confess it. That thought is frightening and proves that we are not yet high enough to uncover the Great Visage, but it will come. All the human and coarse mirrors over which God is leaning, he will break, one after another, until the earth presents himself with one in which he can see his perfect image. Oh, when shall we be pure enough?"

While speaking thus, Adrian had taken Eve's hands, had drawn her toward him, had moved his head closer, and their neighboring mouths were trembling slightly, as if something, unknown to them, wanted to make a single flesh of them.

"Oh!" he groaned, pulling himself together. "Always that enemy within us! Help me!"

And he wept, on the young woman's knees.

It really was amour, of the most terrestrial kind.

They had thought they were mounting toward God, and they fell back at the feet of the Beast, for Nature always thinks of her inexplicable ends, and when she puts a man and a woman in one another's presence, it is always to extract life from them, to make joy and pain, to draw a further exemplar from the obscure Book that never pleases the celestial Reader, and which will represent human being, for millions of centuries, with laborious corrections and successive embellishments, until it is the supreme masterpiece worthy of being read by the eyes of the stars.

VIII. A Bird Sings

Dr. Adrian was not at all discouraged.

He asked Eve to come back. And the initiation continued.

Again they went into the countryside together. They were seen going into the cemeteries of neighboring communes, and making long pauses around those new stones, sculpted in banal fashion, which bear lists of names, which disappear every Sunday beneath flowers, and which represent collective monuments raised to the dead who are not there: the victims of the war.

One day, at the foot of one of those monuments, Adrian confided to Eve one of the reasons, hidden until then, that had retained him in the region.

"The Basques are reputed to be, with the Bretons, the last believers in France. They are still honest, sober and mystical. The new religion can be born here. The future Bethlehem—or Nazareth, since Renan declares that Jesus was born in Nazareth—will perhaps be one of these wretched villages perched on one of these mountains.

"In any case, if a new religion is to be produced, it's here that one has the best chance of observing it.

"Before knowing you, Eve I often came here to interrogate the black-clad peasants kneeling before these monuments to the dead. There is one of them, frequently visited, not far from your house, in the cemetery of your commune, I believe. And that is why I passed so frequently, in the evening, alongside your orchard. I ask your permission to continue now, with you, a certain enquiry that I undertook all alone in the cemeteries of your region.

"It pleases me to question women who are weeping. I talk to them about the son, the husband or the brother they have lost. I try to inspire confidence in them, to win their sympathy, and when I have succeeded in that, I listen to them talk about their dead. Sometimes, I learn important things that way.

"Those dead men, they have the pleasure of often seeing again in their dreams. There are others who believe that they still hold their children in their arms, almost every night. Some of them have confessed that gleams of light appear to them from time to time, which must originate from them; that breath sometimes passes over their faces that can only come from them. And it's probable, in fact, that it is them."

"Oh! You believe that?" Eve interjected.

"Alas, no. I don't believe absolutely, and that is my great misery. But I hope to believe soon. And it's at that formal certainty that I want to arrive, to which I want to guide you. I want, with your collaboration, to prove survival to the world, to convince the most incredulous that nothing more than a page that is being turned in the incomprehensible Book of Life. I want to demonstrate, by means of facts as precise as theorems, the law of Karma that the most noble basis of the Buddhist religion, and thanks to which, as I've told you before, humans are led to do good by egotism, by calculation, since they will be happy or unhappy in their next incarnation according to whether their actions have been good or evil. The day when that moral principle can be established by a plus b on the blackboard of every school, our planet will become once again the terrestrial paradise that it once was. Mademoiselle Eve, it's you who will help me to write on the blackboard, by means of a plus b, the solution to the Great Problem. In the meantime, I ask these poor peasant women in the cemeteries for a little enlightenment."

"And you believe, Master, that peasant women..."

"Why not? I'm convinced that it's always necessary to commence with the humble. It's not in the elegant world, nor among the intellectuals, that Jesus recruited his apostles. I seek information from the poor and the simple because their hearts are more loyally open to visitors from on high. Peasants almost all believe in God and the Devil, sorcerers and ghosts. We call them superstitious, but what is superstition? A distorting mirror, in which the unknown is reflected. We only see grimaces there, but there are also smiles.

"If I've commenced by interrogating peasants about their dreams, it's because the Afterlife is initially manifest to us via our dreams. Natural sleep proves to us that the soul is independent of the body, and provoked sleep, otherwise known as the mediumistic trance, proves to us that our soul can communicate with superior spheres.

"I know that men of science still deny that communication. But men of science once denied magnetism, and the circulation of the blood, and the gravitation of the stars, and everything that hinders them in their habits or might affect their profits. Official scholars are always a century or two behind others. Their ambition is not to set forth for the stars but to sit comfortably beneath a cupola. They are people who know where they are going. Blessed are the rich in intelligence, because the earth belongs to them. But the other world...

"Oh, how you make me ramble, my young friend, Give me your hand for a while so that I can get back to the realm of the Heavens."

Thus they conversed, under the rigid cypresses in the little Basque cemeteries, all situated on the top of hills between earth and heaven, as if to ensure that the dead do not have so far to travel.

One day, in one of those fields of rest not far from Ustaritz, they witnessed a strange scene.

They saw a beautiful young woman detach a red rose from her hair, kiss it for a long time and then deposit it in the monument to the dead near a Basque name: Michel Ellisondo.

A few seconds later, a little hunchbacked woman appeared who picked up the red rose, tore it apart and threw it away. Her fist threatened the beautiful young woman and her mouth uttered a flood of hateful words.

But the beautiful young woman did not seem to be in a humor to tolerate that. She turned to the hunchback and riposted vigorously. They were both Basques; neither Adrian nor Eve understood anything of what they said. But they saw the young woman with the rose suddenly fall upon the hunchback, grab her by the hair, rip her bodice and send her to the ground with a furious shove. The hunchback screamed. Her rival started trampling her beneath her white espadrilles. One might have thought that she was dancing a fandango on a cadaver. Then she readjusted her headscarf, blew a kiss toward the monument to the dead, and departed, laughing.

Eve and Adrian drew closer in order to pick the hunchbacked woman up. She was raging, uttering piercing screeches and pointing to the shreds of her bodice. Such a beautiful fabric! Thirty francs a meter at the Nouvelles-Galeries!

"But why did you want to prevent that young woman from offering a rose to a dead man?" Adrian asked her.

The hunchback replied in bad French, her eyes burning like two firebrands: "She doesn't have the right to offer flowers to that dead man. He was my husband."

"Your husband?"

"Yes, Monsieur. That girl is a brazen hussy. She took my husband when he was alive. I don't want her to continue to take him from me now he's dead. Am I not in the right, Monsieur? And is it also necessary that she insults me, that she beats me, that she tears my clothes? Oh, Monsieur and Madame, there's a God on high and he'll avenge me against that girl, since the gendarmes won't. Oh, the gendarmes, the judges, the rich, they all run behind her skirts. And I'm only a hunchback. But there's a God! There's a God!"

Even and the doctor were moved to pity. It was, however, a tragic situation: a phantom torn between two living women, a wife betrayed even in the other world.

Adrian would have liked to kiss the hunchback's unkempt hair. What could he say to her?

He took a hundred franc bill out of his wallet. "Will you permit me, Madame…for your bodice…Accept it, I beg you…"

The little cripple ceased weeping. A hundred francs. It really was a hundred franc bill.

"Oh, Monsieur!" she said, dazzled.

She seemed ready to kneel down. What did the rival matter, the insults and the blows? What did that persistent and eternal posthumous adultery matter? A hundred francs. For such a sum, could not a pauperess forge all the things of this world and the other?

Adrian was saddened. How easily the woman was consoled!

He thought that he ought to offer her a small moral. "Madame," he advised, "why not offer flowers to your husband yourself? Bring him roses as well. His soul will love you."

"Oh, Monsieur, if that were true!"

"His soul will love you if yours renders itself worthy of it."

"Well then, I'll bring him roses every day. I loved him so much! But he made me suffer so much!"

"Don't forget, Madame, that Christ preached the forgiveness of insults. He said: Love your enemy. If someone strikes you on the right cheek, offer him the other."

"Oh, Monsieur, is it possible that Christ said that? He must not have been Basque...but I repent, since it's bad. I repent of having been so angry. And wait..."

The Basque woman took a few steps toward the nearby tomb, perceived her rival's red rose fallen in the grass, perched it up, straightened it, and came to lay it on the stone in front of her husband's name.

Troubled in spite of herself, Eve said to the doctor: "That's good, what she did there."

And Adrian was also moved. "Worthy woman, that action is agreeable to God. I'm sure that your husband's soul loves you at present, and always will."

"Oh, Monsieur, how I'd like that!"

"I'm sure that it will return entirely to you, that it will no longer pay attention to anyone else, that it will remain faithful to you."

"Oh, Monsieur, if I could believe..."

"Believe!"

Adrian placed a hand on the poor woman's untidy hair.

Then she became transfigured, took the hand of the old scholar, whom she sensed to be so honest, and who resembled the good God of her church, and then kissed it like that of a saint. She believed.

Adrian smiled at her and drew away. He was radiant. Eve was also smiling.

There's a happy woman, she thought. *Henceforth, she'll imagine that she reigns alone over her husband's phantom, that the phantom will no longer betray her. Oh, illusion! Amour to those who spread it over the earth!*

And Eve's cheek posed, involuntarily, on Adrian's shoulder, like a weary ewe against a mossy rock that attracts it.

Adrian had the strength to shrug off that cheek, so soft and odorous—but it was with difficulty.

The evening sun, between two clouds, gilded the tombs. One might have thought that it was kissing them in turn. Why do the living love more readily among the dead? Is it not because the dead tell them that all the rest is vain?

In the direction of the village, a bird sang. Eve and her friend went toward the bird. All songs seemed to them to be appeals.

They emerged from the cemetery and saw the bird. It was a goldfinch. It was singing in a cage. Adrian looked at it.

"Come," he said to Eve. "I'm happy and I want to make others happy. There are wings suffering there. Everything that sings, this evening, is a little bit me. Let's go deliver those wings."

Eve followed him, as the Samaritan woman followed Jesus.

The bird's cage was nailed to the shutter of an inn near a table soiled by wine at which two drunken men were arguing. Above them, the bird was singing, its wings vibrant, its head tilted back, as if it were gargling with sunlight. Sometimes its little eyes swiveled, all white, like those of mediums in a trace who can see prodigies.

The doctor went into the inn.

"How much do you want for that bird?" he asked the innkeeper.

"It's not for sale, Monsieur."

"Name your price."

"There is no price."

"What if I gave you a hundred francs?"

Adrian took another bill out of his wallet.

"A hundred francs?"

The innkeeper was alarmed. The drunks fell silent.

"Bah! Let him have it," proclaimed the voice of a woman who was next to a stove, watching a frying-pan. "We'll easily find another."

A little child began to cry.

The innkeeper unhooked the cage. Adrian deposited the bill on a table and took the bird in his hands. He discovered a small thread of blue silk that the goldfinch was wearing around its neck: the collar of slavery.

"Kiss its wings," Adrian said to Eve.

Then he emerged from the inn, opened his hands above his head, in the direction of the setting sun, and released the bird.

"Go, little one! go live your beautiful life of amour and liberty!"

He gave a few sous to the weeping child and went away, content.

"I'm only a plagiarist, he said to Eve. "It appeared that Leonardo da Vinci did things like that in his fine city of Florence. He ruined himself liberating caged birds and restoring them to the heavens. Heaven repaid him well; it inspired his masterpieces. Let's go. I won't have wasted my day if I've given pleasure to a bird..."

Eve kissed his fingers as she had kissed the wings.

In front of the inn, they were laughing joyfully.

"It's the Madman! The old Madman of Larbouset. You know!"

And the drunks wanted to throw stones at him.

Two days later, Eve and Adrian passed that way again. And in a sunken road, half-buried in the undergrowth, they found a dead bird.

The goldfinch. It was definitely the same one. The trace of the thin ribbon could still be seen around its neck.

The goldfinch…they thought they were securing its happiness, and they had killed it. Adrian went pale. He would have liked to kneel down before the bird and beg its pardon. He remained nonplussed for a few second before the undergrowth, and when he set forth in his route again, he could not dissimulate a frightful discouragement.

"There!" he said. "One thinks one is doing good and one does harm. The bird was denatured. It no longer merited living except in a cage. It no longer knew how to make use of its wings. How many humans are like that, in cages! And I am trying to return their wings! Oh, is it not despairing? And if it were only that bird! But what about the Basque woman, the pitiful woman of that same day? What further sadness! Why demonstrate survival to that women, if the miseries of earth are to continue in heaven? She loves her husband, but what if her husband does not love her? Can you see the soul of Don Juan obliged to lend itself, up there, to the amorous fantasies of the thousand and three? It cannot, however, accord itself to all of them at the same time. And they will all remain unhappy for eternity. That's the reef of spiritualism. One starts from the false principle that two souls united in the bosom of God after death will enjoy an endless happiness. Yes, one of them perhaps. But the other? What quarrels in the azure! Would it not be better, the oblivion that abolishes everything?

"I'm a wretch, Eve. I no longer know what it's necessary to do, I no longer know where it's necessary to go. Everywhere there is good and evil. All causes can be defended one day and combated the next. Were those people not right to believe me mad? And you, are you not going to think that I am? Oh, reassure me, have pity on me!"

Eve took Adrian's head in her hands and kissed his eyes

As was as if the breath of a furnace passed over their napes

"Oh, yes, yes!" he exclaimed. "Perhaps it's there, wisdom! Oh, my God, why go to search for you so far away when you're so close a hand?"

But he was still able to collect himself. He pushed away those mad lips.

"Friend," he said, shivering all the way to the roots of his hair, "that kiss I shall render to you after my death!"

"Master! What do you mean?"

"After my death. Soon. It's time..."

IX. Toward the Stars

Autumn arrived. It is the beautiful season in the Basque country. Eve and Adrian no longer dared venture forth in sunken roads. They took bare paths in order to climb to arid summits beaten by the wind. There they believed themselves to be further from temptation.

Pascalot still followed them, but the arid summits were no more favorable to him, an obtuse animal, than the sunken roads. He became a sheep, and he too went mad. One day, he hurled himself upon Eve, whom he loved, and nearly knocked her over. The proximity of that adult was evidently dangerous. It was necessary to get rid of him—and that was heart-rending for the old man. But could he allow his friend to be killed?

One evening, Adrian took Pascalot and confided him to a neighboring shepherd. He made the man swear that Pascalot would be well cared-for in a stable, that he would neither be killed nor sold.

From time to time, Eve and Adrian went to pay him a visit. The affectionate lamb of old now had horns and had mutated into a bellicose ram. And the transformations of the animal led them to meditate on theirs. Could they oppose the fatal evolution? Would they have the strength to remain pure?

Adrian was getting even thinner. He no longer slept, and no longer ate anything but roots. He wanted to deprive the man in order that the angel might blossom.

Eve was getting thin too. She had thought that she could turn her Master away from vegetarianism, and it was her who had become a vegetarian. Loving Adrian, she contracted all his habits, manias and tics.

She no longer had any concern for comfort or elegance. She no longer wore jewelry, nor silk stockings, not high heels. She no longer travelled by automobile or took any interest in sports. Her former friends did not recognize her. They thought it was some unfortunate passion or even some disquieting malady.

Her father, Melchior Illiberri, the Bayonne banker, became alarmed. He asked her why she was no longer anything but a kind of savage, refusing to go out, to receive, to appear, why she was forgetting so deplorably her duties as a respectable young woman and mistress of the house. There was no longer any means of organizing, at La Floride, a tea or a dinner, any of those charming gatherings without which it is so difficult to prosper and enrich oneself. And if a banker no longer thinks of enriching himself...

Eve was almost never in the house. When she was there she hardly spoke, seemingly absent, no more occupied with her father than with a stranger.

He did not doubt that there was a man in the story. He wanted to know him, and did not understand.

If she had been a minor, perhaps he could have sent her away from La Floride, placed her in a house of retreat or even imprisoned her in a convent. But she was of age and did not seem disposed to quit her Master.

Have her abducted and submit her to doctors who would declare her mad? What a scandal!

Simply cut off her income? Impossible she could be self-sufficient, thanks to the heritage of her mother, who had died a long time ago. Eve was absolutely her own mistress. Nothing could be done against her person. He tried to lecture her, to soften her, to show her the broken family tie, the somber and arid future. Wasted effort.

He presented two excellent parties to her. She declared that she would never marry.

Nothing to be done. The child no longer loved her father, no longer loved anyone except a sort of old madman. All the treasures of tenderness, admiration and respect that Nature had put into that young body were destined for a demented quinquagenarian who was doing God knows what with her.

Was it not a characteristic bewitchment? Occultists, theosophists and mages were reputed to be masters of those redoubtable practices, and Dr. Adrian had the reputation of being a little of all of that.

At the end of a month, Monsieur Illiberri, weary of the struggle, abandoned his only daughter to her severe destiny and sought to assure himself of one more cheerful.

A woman highly fêted in Biarritz, Madame Inès de Beaupréau—a pretty name and a pretty thing—spent a great deal of time at La Floride that season. Monsieur Illiberri was also frequently seen at her home. One stormy evening, the lady thought she ought to sleep at the villa, since there was no hotel in the vicinity. And a few weeks later, she had a room there always ready, even on the most serene evenings.

What could Mademoiselle Eve Illiberri say? She had deserted the house; another had come to take her place.

She wept over it for an entire day, but she went back to Adrian the following day. She was completely subservient to that man. She could no longer live far from him, think about anyone else but him. Where would he take her? What did it matter? To dolor, to dementia, to catastrophe? What did it matter?

A man like him could not inspire a mediocre love. She loved him supernaturally. She had him better than in her flesh; she had him in her spirit. Their ideas espoused one another, voluptuously, in feasts and songs.

At first, she might have thought that she had been pushed toward him by a banal curiosity—such a strange talker!—or even by simple snobbery: that Queen who embraced him. But she had soon realized that it was something else, and that her young woman's body wanted to collaborate with that old man's body in the eternal work assigned to everyone. No champion boxer or football player had ever troubled her like that emaciated and disdainful dreamer.

She recalled their first contact, on the road near the orchard. Then she had been maddened by sun and wind in her precocious apple tree; she was drunk on life, thirsty or sensualities, ripe for embraces. And if hazard had so abruptly attached her to that man, it was doubtless not because she had a presentiment in his society of mental enjoyments and spiritual voluptuousness. She wanted his arms around her waist and his mouth united with hers. And he too, consciously or not, wanted nothing but that from her. All the rest must have been lies, ruses, diplomacy. Nature is wilier than a Talleyrand, and it is to conclude with the work of the flesh that she expends most intelligence. The most mystical song wants the most brutal coupling.

Adrian had ended up taking account of that, for he was increasingly nervous, suspicious and confused. He had the air of an exhausted runner who fears falling on the road. Oh, to forage in the stars when one is only in quest of a bed!

He spoke more rapidly and in a lower tone. He was in haste to finish. He had fixed himself a distant goal, which only seemed accessible after several years, and it was absolutely necessary to attain it in a few months. Oh, how fecund the impending days would be for him!

Adrian took a large exercise book. Into that notebook he copied a host of notes, observations, documents scattered in a dozen small notebooks with which his pockets were generally laden. An on the first page of the exercise book he wrote: *Arrival in the Stars*. That would be the title of his last book.

He worked on it frenetically. Eve surprised him, four or five times, curbed over those wads of paper, his brows furrowed and his eyes haggard, as if the spectacles of Up Above frightened hm.

She understood that it would not be much longer before he let her know the depths of his thought, and reveal to her the nature of the mysterious act that they were to accomplish together, for the happiness of human beings, which would cover them with an imperishable glory.

And, indeed, their relationship took a very different turn. No more vague generalities in their conversations but new and precise particularities. The doctor read his friend studies by William Crookes and Oliver Lodge, the books of Camille Flammarion and Léon Denis. He talked to her about Charles Richet, Colonel de Rochas, Paul Gibier and Lombroso. He explained the theories of the Theosophists and those of the spiritualists. He talked to her about haunted houses and automatic writing, materializations and reincarnations. He revealed to her the names and feats of celebrated mediums, Home, Eusapia Palladino and Mrs. Piper. And finally, he announced to her that he would soon take her to a meeting of occultists.

Often in his correspondence, the doctor found invitations to spiritualist séances or offers from more or less disinterested mediums. Generally, he rejected all that. For a few weeks, however, letters had been pointing to a Basque woman in the vicinity who produced prodigies once a week in the home of a retired customs officer.

The Basque woman provoked apports, and apparitions of hands, heads and entire bodies, so real that they impressed photographic plates. The mold of a hand had even been obtained. Scientists come from Spain had been very impressed. They had given an account of the phenomena in a newspaper in Saragossa.

Adrian resolved to go see all that. The séances took place on Sunday evenings in a chalet in Ciboure, near Saint-Jean-de-Luz. The group was ordinarily composed of seven persons. The medium refused all remuneration. It seemed serious.

To begin with, Adrian went to two séances alone. To the third, he took Eve.

They left for Ciboure one Sunday evening. It was ten kilometers away by easy roads. They went by carriage, an old peasant vehicle, which grated and whined in cadence all along the road, as if it were carrying a dozen crickets in the trunk.

And side by side, silently, fearing the contact of their knees or the brushing of their heads when the jolts maltreated the springs, Eve and Adrian looked at the clouds to search for stars: the impenetrable stars to which have been raised, since time memorial, the eyes of all those who suffer, who love, who doubt, who hope: the eyes of all those for whom the earth is insufficient; the stars toward which an adventurous genius makes a leap from time to time, only to fall back again, with his spine broken.

X. A Spiritualist Group

They arrived. The little town was asleep. The surf of the nearby sea was audible. Owls were calling to one another in the ruins of a church. The lighthouse of Biarritz was parading its circular gaze in the distance. It was cold.

The peasant pulled up in front of an inn; and Adrian led Eve along an uneven side-street. Two or three bends, between low houses separate by shivering gardens.

"It's here," said the doctor," in a low voice.

He stopped before a door and lifted an iron knocker in the form of a dolphin. He struck three raps first, then two, then one. That was the signal. The door was only opened on Sunday evenings to people who knocked like that. All nascent religions surround themselves with mystery. The first Christians celebrated their offices in the catacombs, and the present day spiritualists still celebrate theirs in obscure sanctuaries. One day, perhaps they will have sumptuous cathedrals.

The door opened discreetly. Adrian and his friend went in.

A short corridor, through which the effluvia of onions passed. A cat took fright and disappeared into a stairwell. To the right, a somber door-curtain. The maidservant parted that drapery and ushered the two visitors toward a poorly lit room in which several people were already gathered.

A stooped old man detached himself from the group and came to greet the doctor. That was Monsieur Caliston Bastarrèche, the master of the house: a retired customs officer who had kept watch in the mountains for twenty-five years, who resembled, with is unequal eyes, his twisted mouth and his profound wrinkles, an old tree-stump perforated by woodpeckers.

Few words and few gestures, there was almost no exterior life in the fellow. The other members of the assembly seemed equally unpolished and effaced. By dint of frequenting shades, those living individuals seemed already to be aspirants to the Shadow.

But that had a special gleam in their eyes, as if they were hypnotized by the radiance of another solar system.

The majority of spiritualists are worthy people, virtuous, honest and placid, who accord little attention to the things of this world, only any longer being interested in the other.

Among the women of the group, all clad in black, there was one who stood out by virtue of an exceptionally soft smile. She must have been about thirty. She seemed timid. Her arms were folded and she was hiding her hands on the hollows of her armpits. The others were surrounding her like a Queen, or a fay. And she really was the modern fay, the one who opens, in going to sleep, the doors of the Celestial Tower: the medium.

Briefly, the doctor introduced Mademoiselle Eve Illiberri, who aspired, he said, to spiritualist initiation, and the séance began immediately.

Everyone sat down around a central table resembling an occasional table. The master of the house, who presided over the group, replaced the clear glass of the only lamp with a dark red glass, and a lady recited a special prayer in a clear voice, in which the spirits were invited, in pressing terms, to descend among humans.

When the prayer had concluded, a piano tune resounded in the next room. It was a piece by Mozart, played by the custom's officer's granddaughter, a delicate adolescent who did not yet have permission to practice spiritualism.

Before each séance there was a prelude of that sort: the prayer and the music, as in the mysteries of Allan Kardec. Sometimes, in addition, someone read a page of mystical literature or a religious poem. That, it was said, favored the commerce of terrestrial souls with their siblings in the Afterlife

Beautiful things, in all regions, predispose to great deeds. A masterpiece is a motor, not of a hundred horsepower, but of a hundred archangels. A Holy Chapel has laboratories more powerful than a School of Arts and Crafts.

Everyone was placed in the obscure room, men alternating with women. Eve occupied a chair between the master of the house and Adrian. All the hands were placed upon the edge of the table and joined. No one budged any longer, and no one spoke.

Soon, the table creaked, and then shifted. Eve thought she could feel the roots of her hair catching fire. It was the first time she had seen table-turning; and the sort of sacred terror that everyone feels at the approach of the unknown is already sufficient to demonstrate that the air is populated by phantoms. One is not afraid of that which does not exist.

Eve was trembling.

Adrian asked that they would not attempt, this evening, experiments that would be too distressing.

The president understood. He did not put Cachuca—that was the medium's name—to sleep. When the Basque woman was plunged into a trance, terrible phenomena could be produced. Once, they had seen the table rise up, plunge down upon the assembly, and roll around the room with a terrible crackle of broken furniture; and luminous smoke had been seen to appear, which took on the form of faces with radiant eyes; and hand came to pose on heads, white veils mingles with the lack dressed. Then all of that evaporate silently, and they found flowers on their knees.

This evening, to spare the nerves of the newcomer, they only devoted themselves to a few preliminary exercises. They asked for Lucius, the favorite spirit, the astral guide of the group. He did not come at the first appeal. In his stead, vulgar spirits descended, from which only banalities, incomprehensible or stupid speeches could be obtained. A fake Victor Hugo could not succeed in making a true rhyme.

After twenty minutes of waiting however, the president recognized Lucius by a few clear words of high philosophy transmitted by the vibrant foot of the table. And Lucius announced his imminent reincarnation, which saddened his adherents, for they dreaded no longer receiving his communications.

When Lucius had departed, a lady asked for the disincarnate spirit of her son, who had been killed at Charleroi in 1914. She obtained from him a breath on the forehead, so sweet that she almost fainted.

Caliston Bastarrèche, the president, then said to Eve: "Do you desire, Mademoiselle, to interrogate some cherished individual? Or would you like to communicate with some defunct great man? Pasteur sometimes deigns to converse with us..."

She seemed to hesitate. A great man, a Pasteur, would be very intimidating, but she consent to evoke the spirit of her mother, whose portrait she always carried on her: a photograph already discolored, which represented her at the age of thirty, with a law neckline, smiling, as beautiful as a goddess.

The table soon announced that the spirit of Madame Illiberri was there, and Eve's heart remained oppressed by that, as if it had been suddenly gripped by an ardent fist. She asked, like the previous lady, to feel the breath of the dear departed on her forehead. But she was not very certain of perceiving it. Perhaps she did not have sufficient faith yet.

Everyone knows that a single unbeliever in a group of believers can indispose the spirits and prevent all efficacious communication with them.

That demi-success did not astonish anyone. The president said to the neophyte: "I hope, Mademoiselle, that we can show you more impressive phenomena the next time. There is a commencement to everything."

That was the opinion of the entire group.

Eve and Adrian thanked their host, wished their brothers in Allan Kardec good night, and withdrew placidly.

Eve was not discontented with her evening. Her first contact with the Afterlife had gone quite well. The doors to the Unknown had not yet been thrown wide open, but a thread of light had filtered through a narrow skylight. The great dazzle would be for later.

All the people in the group had left her the best impression. Cachuca did not seem to be a fraud. None of the men seemed to have perceived that neophyte was a pretty girl and none of the women had addressed the slightest compliment to her regarding her hat. Milliners and dressmakers must lose their importance on the astral plane.

At the inn in Ciboure the peasant had stabled his horse and cart. Eve resumed her place beside Adrian behind the driver. A few stars were shining. There was one large one in the west that was sinking into the sea. Eve

182

asked its name. Adrian replied in a weak voice: "It must be Venus."

A few seconds later he felt Eve's hand approaching his own. He no longer defended himself. He accepted the hand, which was naked, and so cool, and so soft. He kept it tenderly in his own. And, with a sigh, Eve thanked him.

Perhaps she was thinking, while the crickets in the trunk and the springs resumed their song, in cadence, in the winter night: *What is there in a hand, then? If it can cause spirits to descend into the wood of a table, what might it introduce into the flesh of another hand?*

Oh, the angels! All the angels on high, do they not come to surround them with their amorous wings, two lovers who are holding hands?

The following Saturday, they returned to Ciboure, to the poor house that reeked of frying and the cat

This time, Eve perceived her mother's breath clearly. She was bowled over by it.

A fortnight later, at the weekly séance, the president put Cachuca to sleep. And the prodigies commenced immediately, at first in complete darkness, and then in the red clarity of a lamp.

Eve heard a harp playing. She saw a flash of light behind a curtain and hands emerging from that curtain. One of them came to offer her a rose. Eve touched the flower and felt it covered with dew.

At the fourth séance, mediumistic writing was obtained. A pencil was placed between two slates placed flat, one against the other. The two slates were tied together with a solid piece of strong; the knots were sealed; the whole was placed under the table, and almost immediately the pencil was heard to scratch. It was so clear that it was possible to divine, by the noise, a *t* being crossed, a period or a circumflex accent being added.

The message was read shortly thereafter, by the normal light of the lamp. It was Lucius, who had come to say adieu to his faithful adherents. He was to be reincarnated, in two days time, on one of the upper plateaux of the Pamir. But in saying his farewells he predicted imminent catastrophes that would terrorize Europe Some members of the audience understood that Bolshevism was about to take over Italy, others that Germany was about to attack France. Fortunate Lucius! On a plateau in the Pamir, he would be sheltered from the torment.

At the fifth séance, the medium having been plunged into a state of profound hypnosis, phenomena of capital importance were produced, which Eve would never forget.

She saw her mother appear. It was terrible and soothing.

Cachuca seemed dead. Her eyes were revulsed, her arms rigid, her body cold. Her heart had almost ceased beating. In order that no fraud should be possible, Adrian was holding her wrists, the president her ankles.

At first a sort of smoke emerged from her garments in the thoracic region. Then that smoke was illuminated, elongated and broadened out. It took on the aspect of an agitated nebulosity. And gradually, parts of that nebula condensed, passing from the fluid state to the solid state. The medium exhaled a disquieting gasp. Then, in the nebulosity, a forehead was sketched, two eyes, and entire face, exquisitely oval, with a seraphic expression. And blonde hair framed its features, dazzling shoulders displayed their curve, a tea-rose appeared between the two breasts....

Eve sighed. She recognized that woman, so blonde, so beautiful, who was smiling at her. It was her mother; her mother at thirty, as she was represented on the familiar little piece of cardboard that she kissed every evening and every morning, which was there, in the little silver locket.

Eve raised her arms and knelt down.

And in her arms she felt the friction of a veil; on her forehead she felt lips. Her mother kissed her... No, no, she was not dreaming; she was seeing clearly, feeling distinctly. Her mother kissed her...

She sighed. She wept. How could she still doubt?

She thought about the portrait of her mother that was there, in her little silver mesh locket. The apparition and the photograph had the same features, the same inclination of the head, the same expression. The coiffure was identical. Impossible to be mistaken. It could not be a hallucination, because all those present saw the same image. And if Eve, by means of autosuggestion, might have reconstituted that faithful image, how could the other people in the group have been able to do so, since they had never seen Madame Illiberri, since they were unaware of the existence of the portrait?

Adrian appeared convinced. All the witnesses shivered, the unique frisson with which the flesh prickles on contact with the Great Mystery.

"Oh, Master!" said Eve, letting herself weep on her friend's shoulder. "Master, it seems to me that I'm reborn, that I'm entering into a new life. Oh, Monsieur le Président, Mesdames, I thank you for having lived that moment. I thank you for having...oh, my God! I..."

Eve's face was transfigured, her voice weakened. Her eyes were seen to revulse, her body to arch...

"Light!" cried the doctor.

Eve fainted.

The president turned up the light, gradually. An excessively abrupt light might have killed the medium.

The phantom evaporated and Cachuca had a violent spasm, as if something were entering into her violently.

Eve's hands were palpated. They were icy.

"I believe," the president said, "that she will be a god medium too."

When Eve woke up, she seemed overwhelmed by fatigue, as if she had come back from a long way away, from a region that the living ordinarily do not penetrate. On a divan, Cachuca seemed even more exhausted. The president prepared her a glass of warm wine. She did not remember anything. And the customary smile returned to blossom on her pale lips, which the blood had reanimated, having been the lips of a corpse a minute before.

That evening, in the small vehicle that took them back to La Floride, Eve remained silent. It seemed to her that henceforth, she would be less able to talk to terrestrial creatures. But her hand remained in her friend's hand, and her shoulder leaned on his. She was happy.

From time to time, a jolt brought the two heads closer for a second, and one of Eve's hairs touched Adrian's ear.

A hair...what is a hair? Such a little thing...but are there any little things? Does not science inform us, every day, that the wing of a mosquito has as much importance as the Milky Way?

It was a cable, that hair; a powerful cable in which a formidable fluid circulated. Eve and her friend thought they were in the ether, departing for the stars; that hair brought them back down to earth. That hair poured an infinite softness into Adrian's flesh. That hair made him vibrate from the nape of his neck to his toenails. That

hair magnetized him, bound him. Would it not be necessary to follow it, that invisible golden thread, everywhere that a breath of wind might carry it? Adrian felt
his heart suspended from that hair like a fish at the end
of a line.

And it must have been saying to him, the subtle hair
that the nocturnal wind was agitating over the neighboring ear: *Poor fellow! You thought you were strong; I am
much stronger. You wanted to remove yourself from the
common path; I will take you back there whenever it
pleases me. You thought you had tamed amour, but you
are its prisoner. It holds you via me. You can run away;
you will not get far. I retain you as a chain retains its
convict. You wanted to escape the laws of nature, you
wanted to be an exceptional being; know that all the exceptional are wrong, and that God punishes them. You
shall see, poor man who has dreamed of being more
than a man...*

The vehicle jolted in the shadow. It stopped before
a gate.

"I believe that you've arrived," said Adrian.

She shuddered. Yes, it was La Floride. It was her
house. Already!

She did not say anything. She turned toward her
Master, looked at him, and then, abruptly, she took his
head in her hands and extended her face, her lips, her
entire being...

What a minute of vertigo!

But Eve recoiled, as if the phantom of her mother
had just interposed itself.

Adrian sighed. That time, he would perhaps have
consented...

He spent a bad night, groaning and stirring. That
hair was still burning his ear.

The following days frightened him. It was the end of March. The heaths were covered with flowering gorse. The hills were decked with golden carpets, as if to receive a god. Birds twittered madly as they pursued one another, and on contact with their wings, an oak, here and there, let its last dead leaves fall, like a philosopher his utopias. It was the most dangerous season of all.

Adrian no longer dared get close to Eve. How little progress they had made in their ascension! Always the Beast, the odious Beast, which hooked them and threw them into the mud.

Eve became more beautiful. Why? There were days when her friend had the temptation to vitriolize her, in order to love her with a divine love.

But is there a divine love? Do not beings who believe themselves capable of it already have the breath of death over them?

It was necessary, however, to continue the initiation.

Adrian was living with his eyes fixed on a splendid goal at the summit of an august peak. Before dying, he wanted to climb it with Eve. But she was not yet sufficiently motivated for that rude climb. She was not sufficiently steeped in occultism, she had not familiarized herself sufficiently with the tempting Afterlife. Oh, on the day when her instruction would be adequate, the day when a complete harmony would reign between them, when their souls would go forth with an equal flight, wings joined, then he would finally be able to confide to her his terrible and courageous project.

Oh, let the Beast grant them mercy for a few more weeks, and they would arrive at the feet of God.

XI. Preparations for Departure

They plunged back frenetically into their experiments, into their studies. The first part of *Arrival in the Stars* was written. They returned to Ciboure. They witnessed disconcerting realizations, multiple incorporations. Every Saturday evening, the Mystery left a shred of its veil in their hands.

When the Basque woman Cachuca was suffering, Eve replaced her. Monsieur Bastarrèche had been right; she became an excellent medium. It only required a few magnetic passes to put her to sleep. One evening, she achieved a trance state, and the apparitions multiplied. One might have thought that all the disincarnate wanted to revive in that splendid flesh.

But Adrian no longer permitted her to dispense herself so generously. It was necessary to husband her resources. Mediums who are abused fall ill or go mad. He needed, for an imminent future, an Eve who was sane and strong. They no longer went to Ciboure except on evenings when Cachuca was to operate.

They requested from that woman the reproduction of all the phenomena related in journals of spiritualism or psychic science, and the majority filed before their eyes.

Adrian repeated the most famous experiments of Crookes, de Rochas, and Lodge. He checked everything that he had found in the books of Lombroso, Flammarion and Léon Denis. He weighed Cachuca while she was asleep, and observed that she was lighter by ten, fifteen or twenty kilos, depending on the degree of spirit materialization. There really was a transportation of substance, an exchange of atoms, between this world and the other. The heavens had visited the earth.

Eve was bowled over by those visions. No doubt could any longer eat into her. She would believe until death.

In the beginning, like everyone else, she had raised a few timid objections. That darkness...why are the majority of the phenomena only produced in obscurity? Is it not to favor the deceptions, the frauds and the tricks of mediums? Are the spirits afraid of light?

But she found, in Adrian's library, very clear explanations for all that. Léon Denis had said: "Every seed, every body, whether it be vegetal, animal or human, must constitute itself in darkness before appearing in the light of day" And Camille Flammarion had cited a laboratory experiment: put hydrogen and chlorine into a vessel; the mixture is conserved if it is left in darkness; but if it is exposed to light, a deflagration takes place and nothing remains in the bottom of the glass but a new produce: hydrochloric acid.

And what about photography, silver bromide? Does it not require darkness in order to reveal to us the image impressed upon it?

Why should the physics and chemistry of the Afterlife not be regulated, like those of this world, by particular laws?

Furthermore, certain experiments have affirmed, for some time, that materializations can be produced in broad daylight.

It was necessary to believe. It became impossible not to believe.

Adrian showed Eve, one evening, that Cachuca's entranced hand could cause the pan of a balance to descend without touching it: an inexplicable phenomenon already produced by William Crookes.

Another evening, he obtained a photograph of a phantom cat, which had just died and was prowling invisibly in the dining room at Ciboure. That discovery did not surprise anyone in the house of the honest customs man, for if one attributes a perispirit to humans, why refuse it to animals? Nature ought to make scant distinction between the species.

Another time, a participant having brought her dog and having kept it on her lap during the séance, the dog was heard to howl mortally as soon as a spirit appeared. That seemed to demonstrate clearly that the apparitions were real and not the result of a collective hallucination.

And Adrian was obliged to conclude, like Sir Oliver Lodge, the rector of the University of Birmingham:

"A conviction of the certainty of the future existence has to me personally been brought home on entirely scientific grounds."[9]

(Annals of Psychic Science, 1897.)

And he was tempted to say, like William Crookes, the illustrious scientist of the Royal Society:

"Spiritualism is officially demonstrated."

And he recalled these characteristic lines of Victor Hugo, a practicing spiritualist:

---

[9] This quotation comes from a public lecture give by Oliver Lodge at St. James Hall in London on 29 March 1897 and widely reported in the press.

The dead are living mingled with our combats
And we feel their invisible arrows passing by...

And he had a desire to go and proclaim to all the mothers and all the widows kneeling in France before thirty or forty thousand monuments to the dead, what Dr. Charazain had said at a recent spiritualist conference:

"Oh, do not weep too much for the dear ones stolen from you, for having known the bitterness of separation, you will know the joy of seeing them again."

If that were true! Why should it not be, since all the world desires it? Could all human beings, in every century, in every land, have been impassioned by a lie?

The argument is only mental, but in all domains, is not the mental in the process of holding sway over the physical?

"Yes, yes, all that is true," said the Master to his young friend, on a day of exaltation when spring as working miracles throughout the undergrowth. "A new religion is in elaboration, in which everyone can believe, and by which everyone will be regenerated. I can hear the footsteps of a Messiah on the other side of the wall. It is going to open, the wall. Let us prepare our eyes and our souls. After centuries and centuries of wandering, humankind is finally emerging from the darkness. At present, it is in the gray, but tomorrow, it will be in the blue; and one day, it will be in the white, in the definitive Light. And after the experiment that I am projecting, and will soon attempt, everyone will be convinced, dazzled. Our love will have made that clarity."

"Oh! How? Explain it to me?" the neophyte dared to ask, again.

But Adrian did not think the time had come yet. He avoided replying. And on one day of prostration, when hailstorms were bruising his garden, he said: "What if it were all false, though? There are so many serious scholars who declare that it's false, who deny everything, even levitation and telepathy. In France three-quarters of the members of the Institut still affirm that there is no immortal soul, that nothing can survive a putrefied body, that annihilation lies in wait for us and swallows us, our actions and thoughts, forever. They certify that mediums deceive us, that all the phenomena only prove one thing: the skill of prestidigitators. And it's true that three-quarters of spiritualists are the prey of brazen simulators. I myself, once...

"*Les Chevaliers de l'Au-Delà*, as I don't know what novelist put it. I knew a fairground conjurer, once, who could reproduce all the spiritualist phenomena on any trestle-table. And I remember a circular written in English from which, for one pound sterling, aspirant mediums could learn the art of deceiving the public, of simulating incorporations, of making phantoms appear, producing apports of flowers, etc. And there are considerable scholars who, without denying the phenomena, explain them by suggestion and thought transmission, certifying that the dead have nothing to do with it. Oh, one gets lost there! Alternately, half the earth is in shadow and the other in the sunlight. Our brains are like that: sometimes night and sometimes day, doubt and faith. Perhaps there are no permanent truths. But what does it matter my friend? After my experiment, the two of us, at least, will know!"

"How?" she asked, again, enervated by such a long wait. "Tell me, finally, how, or I'll think that you're making fun of me? Oh, forgive me! I'm a woman, a curious Eve. You don't want to tell me?"

But Adrian closed her mouth with his hand. And as the mouth persisted, through the fingers, it was necessary to close it—my God!—with his lips...

It was the first time. The results of that kiss were terrible. Eve's entire body seemed to crepitate like a bundle of twigs thrown on the fire.

Adrian got down on his knees. "Forgive me!" he murmured. "The demon is in me, in us...it's necessary to separate, friend, to separate for at least a month. Afterwards, perhaps I shall have the strength to tell you..."

He did not say anything at the end of the week; nothing about that for which Eve was waiting with so much impatience.

He seemed cold, taciturn, almost hateful.

But he began to make strange recommendations, to interrogate her about unexpected matters—her diet, for example.

"Dear friend, what do you eat in the morning?"

"Chocolate, Master."

"In the French style or the Spanish?"

"The Spanish, with cinnamon."

"Good, I shall eat chocolate with cinnamon. And at what time, if you please, do you take that chocolate?"

"At eight o'clock."

"I shall take mine at eight o'clock, then. And in the evening, do you still go to bed at ten o'clock?"

Ten o'clock or ten-thirty, sometimes eleven."

"I shall try to remain awake until then. And you take a bath every morning, I believe?"

"Yes, Master, as much as possible. A bath that is not too hot."

"I shall strive to take one as well, and at the same temperature. But that won't be easy, at Larbouset. And to sleep, do you need a pillow or a bolster?"

"Just a pillow."

"I shall no longer have a bolster, although…"

"But why, Master, do you want to do everything that I do?"

"In order that our bodies and our minds concord entirely. I shall soon need that. It will be necessary for us to have the same regime for everything: for alimentation, for sentiment, for thought. The ideal would be that before any spectacle whatsoever, we pronounce the same words, at the same time, in the same tone. I'd like to arrive at the absolute equality of our reflexes."

"But with what end?"

"You shall soon know. Would you be kind enough to give me your wrist? I'd like to count your pulsations."

"Oh, sixty-five or seventy per minute."

"That's a lot, alas. I only have sixty. That might be where everything breaks down. And your blood pressure? It will be necessary for me to measure it one day. But how do we equalize our blood pressure? How many obstacles there are! For the perfect execution of my project, it's essential that a general harmony is established between us. Oh, why are you so young? Or why am I so old? Thirty years of difference! How can we succeed?

"Will the apparatus of transmission ever be appropriate to the apparatus of reception? Will our muscles or brains and our hearts ever vibrate with the same rhythm and the same amplitude? Problem…"

Eve did not understand any of what he said. Where was he trying to go?

But she obeyed blindly. She was increasingly subjugated.

195

In the hope of finding the key to the enigma, she searched the Master's drawers, doubtless indiscreetly, consulted the notebooks where he had scribbled so many notes, read the first part of *Arrival in the Stars*, where he had explained his doctrine. She did not find anything.

One day, on quitting her near La Floride, he said to her: "At ten o'clock tonight, before you go to bed, will you please be alone and thinking about me."

"I always think about you."

"Think about me forcefully, without distraction, for five minutes. For my part, I will think about you. And tomorrow, you'll tell me if anything happened."

"What might happen?"

"I don't know. Play close attention. At ten o'clock precisely, all right?"

"Very well Master."

They synchronized their watches, and then separated.

The following day, when Eve reappeared at Larbouset, Adrian asked her: "Well, did anything happen? Did you feel anything?"

She blushed. She lowered her eyes.

"A great softness," she replied.

"Be precise."

"How can I be? A great softness. I was happy. I felt you close to me. I would have like to speak to you aloud. I think I even did so."

"Is that all?"

"Yes."

"You didn't feel a need to pick up a pen and write?"

"No," she confessed, "slightly confused."

Adrian seemed vexed. "It's not established," be muttered. "No, truly, the current isn't established. That's very annoying. Still too many dissimilarities! We need to live side by side for ten years, or twenty…but time's pressing."

He had tried to act upon her, at a distance. And he was saddened to observe a failure."

But he persisted, stubbornly.

And after several failures, he registered a victory of sorts.

At ten o'clock on the seventh day, Eve, thinking about him in her bedroom at La Floride, had started to sing.

"What tune?" he asked, radiant.

"What tune? Let's see…I believe it was *Louise*."[10]

"*Louise*. You're sure?"

"Yes."

"Oh," said Adrian, disappointed. "I suggested *Werther*…"

But it was a demi-success all the same. They would do better next time.

And indeed, a fortnight later, at that agreed hour, Adrian having given her a mental order, at a distance of two kilometers, to drink a glass of water, Eve certified the following day that at the prescribed moment, she had felt thirsty, and had drunk a glass of water.

---

[10] Not the popular Maurice Chevalier song of that title, which was not performed until 1929, but the signature tune of the eponymous musical romance by Gustave Charpentier premiered at the Opéra-Comique in 1900, which was an enormous success; it was written with the collaboration of the poet Saint-Pol-Roux, whom Rameau would probably have met at Le Chat Noir when he was a member of the Hydropathes. Adrian's attempted suggestion is an 1887 opera by Massenet, which was added to the Opéra-Comique's standard repertoire in 1903.

Adrian was delighted. The current was finally established.

"I believe that we're there!" he said, squeezing his friend's hand more tenderly. "Our telepathic apparatus is functioning. There aren't any yet at the Post Office."

He became excited His yellow eyes sparkled under their bushy brows. And then, abruptly, he became sad, so sad...

He started speaking to her in a more paternal voice. He wanted to keep her with him longer.

Until then they had scarcely seen one another in the morning. He asked her to come at ten o'clock, at nine, if she could...

She could.

They had lunch together, sometimes at Larbouset, of fruits and vegetables, sometimes in rustic inns, of salads and curdled milk.

They made numerous excursions of that sort along the seashore and in the mountains. And what sweet, new, moving things Adrian was able to say to Eve! It seemed that a poet had been born in him since the day when he had been able to transmit a telepathic order to his friend. In pointing out the most trivial rose-bush in a garden, the merest columbine swaying its mauve flower-heads next to a spring, he had the gesture of a wonderstruck child witnessing the creation of the world.

He became sentimental. He no longer had in his eyes the radiance that commands but that which submits, which pleads which watches over...

How he protected Eve! For her, he was afraid of the sun, of the rain, of the wind. He told her to be careful of cyclists on the roads, to beware of oxen grazing in the meadows. It was evident that she had become infinitely precious to him.

They saw the snow on the mountains melting, as if the sun were harassing them with passionate kisses. They saw the Saint John apple tree becoming weighed down, and recalled a pious anniversary. In certain dells, ferns split the soil like bishops' crosiers, ready to give blessings, giving them the desire to kneel down, to confess.

Oh, the good earth! What would they find, on high, in the promised stars? Can one experience much pleasure before things that one has not see, child? Before things that one has not loved, that one has not mourned? Stars, ought you not to resemble our obscure planet, in order to touch our hearts?

They went forth, they dreamed, they were immensely happy.

They did not speak about amour; they were all amour.

It is not when bees are buzzing that they make honey.

But all the words they pronounced had the sound of amour. They believed they were saying: "See how choppy the sea is!" and they were saying: "I love you."

They exclaimed "Oh, look at that cloud playing hide and seek with the mountains!" and that signified: "I love you."

The thousands and thousands of words of all languages had melted into three.

And they no longer dreamed, he of thinking himself too old or she of thinking herself too young. They were the same age, since they had the same desire. Tenderness is an internal spring, which fills in all wrinkles by infiltration. If Adrian sometimes let some of his show, in the corners of his eyes, they resembled the delicate fractures of books that have been stressed, and which identify stirring pages to new readers. It was good to reread there.

They scarcely quit one another that summer.

Tourists and bathers encumbered the beaches of the area, shooting pigeons here, watching horses butchered there. They went to give salt from the palms of their hands to goat-kids grazing on the heath.

Eve was free. Her father was no longer paying any attention to her. He was probably going to marry the elegant demi-mondaine, Madame Inès de Beaupréau, and that was a fine scandal. But Eve did not seem troubled by it. She let it go. How, in any case, could she have prevented it? Let others arrange their lives as they pleased. Her own was definitively regulated. Wherever Adrian lived, she would live. Elsewhere, the air was no longer respirable.

In their walks, they almost always sought out the heights. The climbed the Rhune together, the Trois Couronnes and the Arsamendi. And that was, for Adrian the lyrical mountain-dweller, an opportunity to recall the influence of mountains on pastors of men. If the earth had not had mountains, would they ever have heard the voices from on high? For the new God, it would be necessary to build a temple on Gaurisankar.

On the mountains of the Basque country, Adrian sometimes seemed to be praying, but he also had strange preoccupations, which troubled Eve on certain days.

He climbed sheer rocks, calculated from above the depths of gulfs that opened at his feet, and generally made the banal reflection: "One could easily kill oneself here."

Why did he say that? What mania, all of a sudden!

Eve drew him away from the mountains and brought him back toward the sea. But she soon perceived that on the edge of the sea Adrian always climbed the steepest cliffs, in order to go along the rim and look over the abysm. And he reflected, aloud: "You know, one could easily drown oneself here."

Oh, what ideas were in his head?

Eve estimated that it was necessary to distract her great friend.

One day, she dared to propose to him: "What if we were to go to Spain?"

"We can't get back from Spain in one day," he objected.

"We could always spend the night there."

"That would be possible for you?"

"Certainly. One night, two nights, a week if need be."

"Well then, let's go to Spain," he agreed. Then, having meditated for a few seconds: "But not tomorrow. Next week. I have so many things to do, before...."

He spent several days putting his papers in order, balancing his accounts, reading the manuscript of *Arrival in the Stars*. And he wrote several mysterious letters to publishers, to relatives, to people of whom he had not had news for years.

"There!" he said to Eve, one evening. "Now, whenever you like."

One might have thought that he was speaking from far away, from the other side of the wall. His eyelids formed a crumpled screen over his eyes, as if something suspect might have been transparent in his gaze.

They left one morning in August, when a heat wave was scaling the plane-trees along the road and the cicadas were crepitating like something frying on a vague ardent aerial stove.

Before climbing into the customary peasant carriage, Adrian had shook the hand of his hostess, the farmer's wife who was always knitting; he had given a small piece of paper to a domestic, kissed a neighbor's child. One might have thought that he was leaving for the Indies.

He took a heavy suitcase. Eve's was much lighter.

To a beggar they encountered, who did not even salute them, Adrian threw another bill. She had never seen him so generous, so emotional.

The railway station was four or five kilometers away, to the north. Nevertheless, he wanted to go in the middle of the day, and that, he said, was to see Pascalot again in passing...Pascalot, the lamb of the previous year, who had been so meek, who had accompanied them on so many walks. What had become of him?

Adrian asked his driver to stop on the stony road two hundred meters from the sheepfold where he had placed Pascalot.

He got down from the vehicle and marched toward the sheepfold along a path bordered with gorse. Eve followed him without saying a word.

Adrian met the shepherd in front of the gate to a field and asked him for news of his sheep.

"Your sheep?" replied the man. "He's well."

"Can I see him?"

"If you wish."

"It's this way, I believe?"

"Of course. Go ahead."

And the shepherd escorted Adrian to the park. Eve was still following, at a distance..

The man opened the large door of poorly-joined planks, which had a flap of dead fern at the top, to stop the flies getting in. The sheep, glad to see the daylight, uttered varied bleats: the imperious voices of adults, the voices of young ones, s tender. Bells hung around necks tinkling. Adrian touched a few woolly backs.

"Which one is he?" he asked the shepherd,

"Perhaps this one...yes, definitely this one."

"Impossible. He doesn't recognize me."

"Well then, it's this one, for sure."

"That one? He doesn't recognize me either."

And Adrian called, in all directions: "Pascalot? Pascalot?"

The name did not disturb any animal.

"Well," said the shepherd, "how can he recognize you after all this time? How long ago is it since you left him with me? Eight or ten months? Put yourself in his place! Anyway, you don't recognize him either, and you have as much brain as he has, that being said without comparison. But I swear to you that I haven't sold him, Monsieur. Look, me, I'm straight in business dealings; if you want him back, you can choose between these two. I swear to you, by the living God, that he's one of these two."

Eve had approached in her turn. She too called: "Pascalot!" And no sheep turned its head at that voice. She could have wept.

Time had done its work. Pascalot, the good Pascalot, who had eaten so many green peas on the knees of his first master, who had gone to sleep so many times on the dress of his first mistress, had forgotten master and mistress alike, who had also forgotten him. The cruelty of passing days, nibbling the heart...

Adrian went back, melancholy, followed by Eve, who dared not speak.

"Well, let's go see your apple tree," he proposed, finding himself back on the stony road. Your Saint John apple tree. Do you remember?"

Did she remember! They days had nibbled away nothing, on that side.

They climbed back into the carriage, and a few minutes later, they were skirting the wall of the orchard, a hundred meters from the villa.

They got down from the vehicle again and opened the unpainted gate.

For two minutes they walked over the cut grass, between the trees. Adrian looked at the trees. He did not recognize the Saint John apple tree either.

"It's this one," said Eve, approaching the wall. And her voice quivered with emotion.

Adrian sighed. The beautiful apple tree, the unforgettable apple tree that he had once called the Tree of Life and Death, the Tree of the New Science. In this season, the tree had no fruit. No asp was paying court to it. It had the sadness of a discrowned king.

Adrian looked at it, but not for long. His eyes became troubled.

He cut a thin branch, which bore three dull, perforated leaves, already ripe for the final fall, and he insinuated the twig into his buttonhole.

Even felt troubled. Why had her Master wanted to see that tree again before going to Spain? Why was he saying his adieux like this to so many people, animals and things?

He had the air of a poor man who is putting his clothes, his memories and all his treasures into a bag, and who is going away, without knowing where, with his bag over his shoulder.

Near the gate, Eve took Adrian's arm. "What are you hiding from me?" she asked.

"Me? Nothing."

"Yes. Show me your eyes. Oh, how moist their gleam is today!"

"It won't be tomorrow. There will be sunlight in them tomorrow, in Spain."

"Let's hope so!"

"Come quickly, friend! We're going to miss the train."

XII. The Voyage to Spain

A quarter of an hour later, they took the train to Irun.

It was a very slow train, which idled between the hills as if it had something to say to all the houses in the region. It stopped here and there under various pretexts: points, work on the track, bends, and also perhaps to catch its breath, for the machine had a terrible asthmatic cough.

But Adrian did not complain about that slowness. The landscape was beautiful: wooded hills, lush meadows and sometimes a corner of the sea plunging into the land like a white nudging elbow. Oh, let the train dawdle! They would be in Spain soon enough.

Adrian did not say anything. He looked at all the things in the surroundings with empty eyes, as if terrestrial horizons no longer existed for him. But from time to time, he welcomed with a sigh the gloved hand of his companion, which wanted to nestle in his own.

"Oh, say something, I beg you!" she implored. "Are you in pain?"

"Me? No."

"What, then? Look how beautiful Fontarabie is at the foot of its mountain. What arrogance it has! That black château, those old houses…it crushes the French coast Hendaye bows down too low before that Spaniard. It's humiliating. And that bell-tower up there! It seems to be challenging us. Oh, no, in this corner one isn't proud to be French. But you still aren't saying anything! Master, why are you silent?"

In an affectionate but toneless voice he replied: "The Orientals have a proverb: Noise is for humans, Silence is for gods."

"But we're not gods!

"We shall be...and soon."

"What do you mean, soon?"

He did not say any more. And his empty eyes continued looking into the distance.

At Irun, they went into a random hotel situated in the middle of the town: Funda da Madrid. They had lunch in the shade of a dusty arbor, the roses of which had to cede to the perfumes of warm oil and garlic.

They mostly ate fruits.

That part of the town being banal, they put their luggage in a carriage and had themselves taken to Fuentarabia. They found an isolated hotel there on a hill: Funda de Sol. The location pleased them. They reserved two rooms, one on the first floor overlooking the sea, the other on the second on the side of the mountain. Adrian took the latter.

And immediately, he wanted to go for a walk, to follow a little road that ran alongside the sea on the Spanish coast. They walked a long way, for an hour, in the direction of Cap du Figuier, the extreme tip of the Jaizkibel.

Adrian was still gazing at sheer rocks, particularly those that were closest to the sea. But he did not find any that suited him. Appearances were deceptive at a distance.

Finally, he perceived one, in the distance, which pleased him. He left the road and went toward the rock along an insecure path, over landslides. Eve dared not follow him.

After a few minutes of exploration, he seemed satisfied. Eve rejoined him, hesitantly, somewhat troubled.

"What are you doing here?" she asked hm.

"I'm looking for a nice place, and it seems that I've found one. Look!"

He showed her the bright estuary of the Bidassoa, the entire caress of the blue water toward the blue mountains. He showed her the French coast opposite, the ruins of Fontarabie to the right, the open sea to the left. Hendaye was displayed on French soil around its squat bell-tower. Over the immense beach—a curved border of the finest gold—the Moorish casino showed its gray colonnade. A pointed mountain, the Rhune, was hooded by a stormy cloud. The two crags, the Twins, pricked beneath the new Château d'Abbadia, not far from the sanitarium, were the landscape's two beauty spots; and a rim of foam around them showed them, like a froth of pleasure, the incessant emotion of the sea.

Eve gazed at all that, The scenery had grandeur and grace, but there were more beautiful spots on that rocky outcrop of the Jaizkibel, notably on the Guadeloupe road, which was nor very far away—except that that road did not overhang the sea.

"It's not bad," said Eve, "but it's dangerous. A gust of wind or a vertigo could throw us into the sea. Let's not stay here, Master."

"How fearful you are!"

"I'm prudent. Come."

Adrian did not obey. He no longer appeared to be listening to her. He installed himself on a damp rock and indicated a narrow ledge beside him.

"Don't you want to come and sit next to me?" he invited.

How could she have resisted? It was said in such a humble, touching voice. She sat down next to her Master on the hard rock.

From time to time a wave reared up toward them, and then, breaking, threw salty mist in their faces.

Adrian seemed glad to feel the rock tremble beneath him.

After a few minutes of silence, in which nothing could be heard but the confused respiration of the sea, he went on, dully:

"Eve, if I've brought you here it's to tell you certain things that you wouldn't have understood as well in a hotel room, or on that disagreeable road where there were so many cyclists. There are confidences that one can only make in certain places, with a very pure sky overhead."

"I'm listening to you, friend."

Adrian gazed at the rocks, the ocean, the boats with gray sails, the villages with pink roofs, with a circular glance, like a fisherman casting a net.

"Here's a piece of paper for you, my dear Eve. Please agree to it. It's my testament."

"Your testament?" she protested. "Why are you thinking about that?"

"It's necessary to think about it at my age."

"But you're full of life!"

"Does one ever know? Then again, there are people who make their testament at forty, thirty or twenty-five. I'm approaching sixty. I haven't left it too long. My dear friend, look after that envelope carefully. You'll read its contents one day if you don't want to read them right away. Let me tell you that, apart from a few objects of no importance, of which I've disposed in favor of half a dozen relatives or old friends, it's to you that I've bequeathed everything I possess."

"Oh, but I refuse. I hope to die before you!"

"No, you won't die before me. That would be neither natural nor acceptable. It's necessary that I depart first, if only to prepare a good place for you on high, for I'd like to believe that we'll find one another again one day and that we shall be as closely united in eternity as we have been for the last fourteen months."

"You're making me feel ill. Don't talk about it anymore."

"It's necessary to talk about nothing but that."

"Look at the sea and the mountains."

"The moment has come to look higher than those mountains."

"But you're frightening me."

"Eve, I beg you to listen to me and to rejoice, for I'm reaching the goal. One more effort and I'll have finished my work."

"What work?"

"I've talked to you about a certain enterprise that I once conceived, and that I hoped to bring to a conclusion with you. This is the moment. I'm not able to put it off any longer. In a few hours, everything will be done."

"What do you mean, Master?"

"I'll explain to you soon, probably this evening. It will be better, I think, that it happens in the evening, for all sorts of reasons. In the meantime let me comment on the intentions that I express summarily in that letter. I have no fortune. I'm bequeathing you almost nothing, scarcely fifty or sixty thousand francs of annual income that I draw from my books, but which will diminish rapidly in four or five years, perhaps sooner. I only have one work still to publish. I'd like it to keep the title, *Ar-*

rival in the Stars, that I've already given it. You know that the first part is completely written. You'll find the manuscript in the drawer of my table at Larbouset. For the second part, I have documents and notes. I beg you to assemble them. Those papers are in the second drawer. There are things that I believe to be interesting in a little green notebook. Please complete all that by means of the personal experiments that you will soon have the opportunity to carry out, at Ciboure or elsewhere. If necessary, for the drafting of that final part, one of my former collaborators will aid you. You'll find his name in my testament.

"Friend, I forbid you…!" Eve tried say, tearfully.

But he pushed away the nervous arms that tried to knot themselves round his neck, and the gaze that he posed on Eve was as penetrating as cathode rays. She felt explored to the marrow of her bones.

"Will you be worthy of the mission that I have confided to you?" he asked, severely. "Will you betray me too?"

"Oh, you know that I'm yours, that you can ask anything of me, that you have only to make a gesture and I'd give my life for you."

He looked at her again and his eyes darkening.

"Perhaps I'll ask you for more than life, my child."

"What, then? Oh, speak, I beg you."

"This evening," he retorted, getting to his feet abruptly.

"Always evasions!"

"No, this evening, I promise you. Oh, how we will love one another in the bosom of God! Come, these waves are temptresses. Come, my young Self, for you are a little bit me already, and you will soon be all of me—at least, all of me that remains on earth…"

"Everything you say is so frightening."

"Come, come! Let me take your thoughts from that pretty forehead. Let me make them mine forever!"

He placed one of his hands on the young woman's head.

She shivered, and followed him, tamed, as if at the end of a chain.

"This evening, after dinner, we'll come back here," he said. The place is good. At ten o'clock, we'll have the high tide. All will go well. You'll come, won't you, my young Self?"

She replied, in a breath:

"Yes, my great Self."

XIII. The Great Experiment

A strange dinner!

There was a basket of white roses on the tablecloth. What betrothal were they celebrating?

There were delicate dishes and select beverages: meat and wine. Yes, although drawn up by Adrian, the menu included meat and wine. What did that debauchery signify?

But no matter how he tried, he could not succeed in eating or talking. The chicken wing stuck in his throat and the witticisms did not emerge. Thus, in winter, next to fountains, the statues have drops of ice on their lips.

When Eve spoke to him, Adrian shivered as if he were coming back from another world. Never had he seemed so absent, so disquieting. She feared an imminent crisis.

He gave a forty franc tip to the waiter.

As he got up from the table, the waiter remarked: "Monsieur has forgotten to offer Madame the champagne.

It was true. The champagne had not been uncorked.

Adrian sat down and filled two glasses. Eve did not touch hers but Adrian drank. He had not tasted champagne for twenty years. He hoped to get drunk. But in his cranial cavity the same ideas were whirling, still precise.

With a nervous hand he took a rose. Then he stood up, energetically, as if he were departing for an attack.

"Let's go!" he said. "It will soon be ten o'clock. It's time."

He took Eve's arm and went away, in the warm shadow, toward the invisible sea, whose breath could be heard.

He headed toward the cape, along the deserted road that they had explored a few hours earlier.

She felt her friend's shoulder trembling against her own.

Where are you taking me, then?" she dared to say.

"You know very well: to the rock."

"What rock?"

"The one from before."

"It's too dark. And you can see that a storm is threatening. There's wind and lightning."

"What does it matter?"

"The sea is high. Our rock will be battered by the waves."

"So much the better."

"Master, I'm going to disobey you."

"Oh?"

He stopped. He looked at her. She sensed the burn of his eyes and lowered her head.

"No, no, Master. I can't disobey you. Go wherever you please. Do with me whatever you please."

"I shall make you an immortal woman," he said, taking her arm again authoritatively.

And he drew her toward the coast, whose somber jagged outline was displayed from time to time by a flash of lightning.

"An immortal woman?" said Eve, astonished. "How will you make me an immortal woman?"

"By giving myself death."

"Master!"

"The moment has come."

"That, then, is what you had to say to me?"

"Yes, that's it."

"What madness!"

"I expected that. But you won't prevent me. The moment has come and I'd be a criminal to wait any longer. Tomorrow, I'd not longer be able to…I shall die tonight."

"Madman! You really are mad!"

"I've never been more lucid. For thirty years, I've only been living for this moment. I've told you a hundred times: I've resolved to do something great extraordinary, decisive, for the good of humankind. I needed a sure fried for that, and I've chosen you. I'd like to believe that you're not going to run away at the last moment."

"But Master…."

"Eve, listen to me! Understand me! I'm going to kill myself in order to demonstrate to the world that I shall still exist after my death…"

"Oh my God!"

"…Kill myself to demonstrate to everyone that death does not exist. And I shall prove it by communicating with you. I shall speak to you, I shall appear to you. I shall tell you what there is in the other world and you will tell people. You will convince them that the soul survives, that it is immortal, that it is recompensed or punished in accordance with the good or the evil that it has done on earth, as the doctrine of the spiritualists teaches. And you will thus accomplish, for the moralization of human beings, the most beautiful action that any woman has ever attempted. You will be their consoler. They will bless you, they will deify you. Thank to you, the Great Torment will cease. There will be no more great despair, no more great afflictions. Millions of mothers, wives, daughters and sisters who have lost a beloved individual in the war will be appeased, since they will have the assurance of seeing that beloved individual again one day. Oh, how beautiful life will be, thanks to us! I shall be the modern Adam. You will be the definitive Eve, the one who offers the fruits of the Tree of Good and not the Tree of Evil; and humans, purified, will raise temples to us in their heart."

"O my great Me, I hear you and I admire you, and I approve of you..."

"So?"

"But if you die, how do you expect me to live?"

"You will live because I have ordered you to, because the salvation of humankind demands it."

"Oh, no! I sense clearly that I won't be able...."

"You will be able! And you will be recompensed for it, my love. Do you hear me? I'm saying to you, *my love*. My heart is finally bursting. For I love you, I love you. And tomorrow, I would be incapable of completing my work."

"Why do it? Let's love one another!"

"Shut up!"

"Why do it? What if you're mistaken? What if everything finishes after death, as so many people believe?"

"Shut up?"

"What if you're about to kill yourself for nothing?"

"Don't say that! It's necessary to believe, Let me depart with all my confidence!"

"But you yourself..."

"I know. I've sometimes doubted. And how could I not doubt? So many different theories and contrary philosophies demonstrate survival for some scholars—believers in the spirit—and do not demonstrate it for others, the positivists. What some attribute to disincarnate spirits others attribute to forces as yet undefined,

216

and what is explained here by the intervention of souls is explained there by suggestion, telepathy, the subconscious. Oh it's enough to break the head! And I'm going to break mine, solely to know."

"And what if you know noting?"

"I shall."

"What assures you of it?"

"According to my calculations, there are two probabilities against one in favor of my knowing, and for my being able to let you know. I've gone so deeply into these matters. Men like Myers, Lodge, Crookes, Richet and Léon Denis cannot be entirely mistaken. I have confidence. We really are immortal, and responsible, and *en route* for a better future. Humans really have departed for the stars, and thanks to us, my love, they'll arrive there sooner."

"What proves that to you?"

"Nothing and everything. I hear the God that affirms it within me; and that is worth more than the negation of so many blind men."

"I've heard mention of other men who have done what you want to do, who have killed themselves in order to have communication with the living thereafter. Even recently—an American, I've read. And what good did it do, that suicide of an American?"

"One can't know so soon. He might have been able to recruit faithful followers, favor propaganda, redouble the zeal of seekers. Deeds like that are never futile. America is already colonized by the spirits. It's theirs. And the proof is that Edison, an official scientist, is trying to construct, so it's said, a strange apparatus, a machine to contact the Afterlife. But what patent assures us that that machine will be well constructed and able to contact the Afterlife? If Edison fails, it will prove nothing. For its part, England is also seeking.

"An agency functions on the other side of the Channel, under the name of Julia's Bureau,[11] which puts the living in contact with the dead. Perfect! When a desperate individual, in England, want to see a cherished individual who has just died, he is referred to a medium who procures him that joy! And no remuneration is requested, which proves that the people are of good faith, serious and convinced. In France there is nothing similar.

"France is the most backward of countries with regard to the psychic sciences. Our writers of vaudevilles, who believe that spilled salt, broken mirrors, three lights and thirteen guests bring bad luck, still mock turning tables, mediums and fluids. It's pitiful. Well, we shall open the ideas of the French; we shall force them to believe. My death will make them reflect—my death and the messages that I shall send you after my death. If the American has failed—which is not certain, it's because he had not taken sufficient precautions. I have taken them, and you have seen them.

"Oh, my love, do you understand why I have done so many things, who I have turned you away from the

---

[11] Julia's Bureau was founded in April 1909 by the journalist W.T. Stead, who announced its existence in an article entitled "The Exploration of the Other World" in the May 1909 issue of his *Fortnightly Review*. "Julia" was allegedly a spirit on the Other Side—and American journalist named Julia Ames, who had died in 1891—who asked for the bureau to be set up in letters transcribed by a friend of hers named Ellen in 1892-3. The letters were originally published in the periodical *Borderland* and were then reprinted in a book, *After Death*, in 1905. The Bureau only existed for three years.

world, why I have retained you in my desert, why I have applied myself to elevate your mind, why I have begged you to be a vegetarian like me, to live exactly like me? It was important, for the success of my plan, that we have the same habits, the same tastes, the same thoughts; that our vibrations be equal, that our spirits be fraternal. There is no certain communication between two different beings. It is necessary, as I've already told you, that the transmitting apparatus and the receiving apparatus are in conformity and well established in regard to one another.

"That is why I have treated you as sibyls, druidesses and vestals were once treated, all the pure young women destined to the cult. And I believe that I've succeeded, Eve. My body and my soul are related to yours, the harmony between us has become perfect, and posthumous communication can be established. And imagine the consequence!

"My suicide will be resounding, since I'm an author of some celebrity. The world will know for what noble cause I have disappeared. It will no longer be some spiritualist or an obscure theosophist who has conceived the courageous enterprise but a man whose books have had success, who has to be taken seriously. My death might be the signal for the Great Revivification...

"Eve, we have arrived. Here is the rock that overhangs the sea, at high tide. I've looked hard. One dive—and all will be said."

"Shut up!"

"Eve, I will love you from on high, and with a love so great that it will have no name on earth. Oh, all that I have not been able to give you during my life, I will give you after my death, and the angels will be jealous of your happiness."

"Friend, I love you too, Stay with me!"

"No. I can't any longer."

"Only love me as I merit being loved! Love me with a terrestrial love, as everyone loves. Oh, that would also be good!"

"Shut up, I beg you! I know that it would be good! Too good, to begin with! But what would become if it, our poor love? What becomes of all love on earth: the mud, after having been the light."

"Oh! No!"

"After a few months, we'd be blasé."

"No! No!"

"After a few years, we'd be indifferent."

"That's impossible."

"Perhaps we'd end up hating one another. I'm over fifty. A man of that age has never been loved for long by a young woman. I'd horrify you. There would no longer by any harmony, any concordance between us. I would no longer be able to attempt the proof, for the spirits on high don't descend toward those who have forgotten them. I've reflected hard! This evening! It's necessary that I die this evening, for my happiness, for yours, for that of living hosts and those yet to be born. *À bientôt*, Eve!"

"Oh, my God! But I'll scream, call for help, beg someone to stop, to lock you up..."

"*À bientôt!* There's the rock, the sea, the stars... Look! Do you see them, the stars? Look: a shooting star...and another...and another... The tears of Saint Laurence, the people say. Look! The stars are flying, descending, falling...they're coming to search for me. I wanted to go to them; it's them that are coming to me..."

"To tell you to stay on the earth!"

"No, to take me and carry me away. Eve, tomorrow, in your orchard, go and kneel beneath the Saint John apple tree. I'll try to make you sense my presence. How? I don't know. Take something with which to write. And if you don't receive any communication tomorrow, come back the day after, come back until I reveal myself! Perhaps it won't be long. And if I can't reveal myself under the apple tree, wait for me in your bedroom, wait for me with our friends in Ciboure in the customs officer's house, around the table. Put the medium into a trance—and I'll come. I'll come, I'm sure of it. And the world will know; it will believe; it will become good again; it will be saved. Eve, I embrace your soul."

He hugged her against his chest. She knotted her arms around him.

"Your soul, Eve. Nothing but your soul..."

"I also have a body!"

"I can't see it."

"It can see you; and I can feel you; and it doesn't want you to die."

"Eve, don't commit this crime."

"It's you who are committing one. Suicide is a crime. All religions, all societies, condemn it. If you have the infamy to kill yourself, the spirits will turn away from you."

"No, my friend. The spirits know that my intentions are pure, and they'll forgive me. The Great Master will absolve me, since I will have worked for his triumph, to bear witness that he exists and that he judges, that he punishes and recompenses. I shall be the best of his apostles. One does not chastise an apostle. *À bientôt*, my love! Unknot your arms."

"No!"

"I beg you to do so!"

221

"No! If you throw yourself into the sea, I shall throw myself in too."

"But are you mad?"

"Yes, for having listened to a madman."

"Eve, love me! Obey me! Don't turn me away from my duty. Think of all the happy people we're going to make."

"Above all, you'll make one unhappy one."

"Oh, I, who saw you so beautiful...you'd be making yourself ugly, Eve. You'd make yourself ugly with your evil action."

"That doesn't matter to me."

"Let me die."

"Not without me. I love you."

"No, you hate me. You hate everyone. You hate God..."

"I love you."

"Eve, in the name of your mother, whom I rendered to you one evening..."

"I love you."

"Well, then...."

Adrian tried to put his hand on her head, in order to tame her, to put her to sleep as before. But this evening, she resisted. No fluid could defeat her. And still, her obstinate voice, which had become dull, said:

"I love you, I love you!"

Adrian no longer hesitated. He gathered all his strength, separated his friend's arms and shoved her aback against the rock.

She collapsed, but she was still able to say: "I love you..."

Then she no longer moved.

Adrian leaned over her, and heard her sobbing.

For a few seconds, she writhed on the rock, delirious, uttering inarticulate plaints, like an animal whose throat has been cut.

Then she became completely motionless. She must have fainted.

Then Adrian took her in his arms again and marched toward the road, tottering, over the rockslides.

He was panting. His courage was at an end.

He saw the headlights of an automobile arriving round a bend, which was descending toward Fontarabie.

He shouted at the vehicle, and gesticulated, begging it to stop.

"Messieurs," he said, on seeing two men coiffed in caps, "have pity on a young woman who has just fallen ill. If you can take her in your auto and have her cared for…there are no houses nearby. I believe she's staying at the Funda del Sol. I found her unconscious on the road. Perhaps you're French? I believe she's French…"

The travelers had got out. Eve had, in fact, fainted. Her body had a cataleptic rigidity. They loaded her into the car. Then, seeing the stranger hesitating:

"What about you?"

"Oh, me…I'm going in the other direction," Adrian replied. And he pointed in the direction of the cape.

"But…all this seems rather shady…get in!"

"Impossible, Messieurs. There's nothing shady about it, believe me. But what is obvious is that this unfortunate young woman needs help. Hurry up! Have a good doctor care for her. God will be grateful to you."

The two men darted another glance at the unknown man, and then shrugged their shoulders, muttering. "Let's go, quickly!"

One took the steering-wheel again, the other sat beside him, and the automobile headed for Fontarabie at top speed.

When it had disappeared, Adrian knelt down on the road. "Great Master of all, forgive me!" he said, raising his arms toward the heavens.

For an instant, he looked at the stars: the fixed stars, which were shining harshly, like metal nails, and the shooting stars, which were detaching themselves gently, like pearls from a necklace whose string has broken.

Then he stood up again, ran to the rock, found the chosen spot, and threw himself into the sea.

XIV. The Afterlife and the Life Before

Blackness.

Vague things, suspect, intermingled, inextricable.

Blackness.

Confused sounds, incomprehensible rumors, shrill voices.

Blackness.

Furtive impressions, fragments of thought, shreds of vision. Who's speaking?

And blackness again.

Sleep, dream, oppression, suffering. Oh, that lead over the nape of the neck, over the heart, over everything.

No, it's no longer as black.

Anguish, fear, frissons, vertigo... What's that sharp perfume that drills into the brain. Are the eyelids stuck, then?

Ah! Whiteness!

There are white walls, white beds, white curtains, white napkins. And in the midst of all that, a white cornette.

"Como se llama usted?"

Who said that? What does it mean?

Blackness again,

Lugubrious, dolorous and frightening, it's said, is the passage from this side to the other side. Abrupt, the shores of the Afterlife. But is this the Afterlife or the Life Before?

Blackness.

"No quiere decir me, usted, como se llama?"

That voice becomes sharper. He plunges back into the blackness, expands into the blackness. He...

The personality returns. One is someone again.

Black, gray, russet.

Oh! Sunlight! It really is the sun! And how it resembles that of earth!

Adrian opens his eyes again. He is Adrian, as before. He opens his eyes and sees a big, big window, which is letting in golden sunlight. He sees a hospital ward. He sees a nun.

"Sister!" he murmurs, spontaneously.

"Ah! Is a Frenchman!" says the voice under the cornette.

And that cornette draws away.

How bizarre it is! There are also nuns in the other world, then? In the other world, there are also iron beds, sheets, blankets, and chairs in the same style as on earth? And in the other world there are beings conformed like those on earth? Hirsute and bald, thin and fat? And there are holy water fonts and crucifixes, as on earth?

What! Crucifixes...

But this must be a dream. When disincarnating, terrestrial spirits carry with them, no doubt, a few residues of materiality, as a butterfly might carry a little detritus of its caterpillar...

Adrian slides back into the russet, the gray, the black. He goes to sleep again. Nothing exists any longer, neither the Afterlife not the Life Before. There is only a milieu, which one fills. That's good.

Blackness.

Ah! There's no sunlight any longer. But there is a cornette. Except that it isn't the same one.

"Well, Monsieur, how do you feel?"

Strange.

Is French one of the languages current in the After-life?

"It appears that you're French? So someone came to look for me to keep you company. Are you thirsty? Here, drink a little. It won't do you any harm."

Adrian is stupefied. He listens, looks, reflects. And he is afraid that he understands...

"Tell me, Sister...?"

"Speak, speak!"

"How did I get here?"

"Oh, I'm no better informed than you are. I've heard tell that you were fished out of the sea in the direction of Fontarabie or the Passages a few days ago, and that the fishermen who picked you up in your boat, not knowing who you were, brought you here."

"Where's here?"

"The hospital of Saint-Sébastien."

"Oh?"

"Worthy fellows, those fishermen. You owe them a fine candle."

"Oh?" Adrian says, again. And his eyes fill with tears, and his temples are covered with sweat.

He has understood.

The nun tries to give him a spoonful of the potion, but he refuses...and he sighs, shivers and turns his head away in order not to see the daylight.

After a further somnolence, perhaps of a few minutes, perhaps of several hours, he opens his eyes again.

It's dark. There is no longer a cornette beside him. Everyone seems to be asleep in the vast room. A rhythmic snoring is rising from a nearby bed, like a bumble-bee passing back and forth.

And Adrian meditates: *I'm not dead. I'm still a poor man. It's frightful. I've been pulled out of the sea, saved in spite of myself. What about Eve? What's become of her? Cured? Dead? What if she's the one who's dead? Eve!*

Adrian's upper body rises up. A cry emerges from his throat.

Promptly, a cornette reappears, which precipitates toward him, puts him back under the covers, maintains him motionless, pressing down on his shoulders. And incomprehensible words resound in the silence.

Adrian gradually calms down and reenters the blackness.

Days, nights. Hours of lucidity, hours of trouble...

He really is mad now; entirely mad.

He realizes that sometimes, on seeing the vigorous men that are summoned to hold him down, and listening to the reflections of the French nun who comes back to see him from time to time.

He is mad, and ill, and so weak! Doctors examine him, lifting up his eyelids, testing his reflexes, shaking their heads. He is nourished artificially. He is no more than skin and bone. But he can still call out: "Eve?"

Many days and many nights.

One morning, he sees the sunlight again, the beautiful new sunlight, which flattens out on the white bed like a warm and silent animal.

Adrian thinks about Pascalot, and he weeps. He remembers Eve, and he weeps.

"I'm cured. I want to leave," he says one evening to the nun from France.

But she smiles. All madmen are like that. They think themselves cured and want to leave.

In any case, Adrian senses himself that he could not leave. He has so little strength! When he puts his foot on the ground, he trembles.

He is questioned again about his name, but he doesn't reply.

They would like to know where he is from, how he fell into the sea, whether it is necessary to alert some relative. No, he doesn't reply. If anyone knew his story...for a start, they would laugh, they would no longer doubt his madness. It's better to keep quiet.

However, he really would like to write to Eve...

Days, weeks, perhaps months.

One morning, he perceives that he had been moved. He is no longer in the same bed, in the same ward. He has been transported to a little room. He is all alone there. Why? Because he has become dangerous to his neighbors, perhaps? And he certainly feels, from time to time, that he is not a normal being, that he gesticulates, cries out, threatens...

Is he going to remain mad, then?

But there are also changes in the light, in the temperature. The sunlight no longer has the same ardor. It must be autumn, or even winter. Yes, through that window, he can see a tree devoid of leaves. Winter...

How many months has it been, then?

And out there, Eve?

He is sleeping better now; he is eating better; he accepts meat, he is putting on weight, recovering strength. His head no longer spins when he stands up. He is cured.

Certainly, he is cured. He can reflect. He can respond to the nun; he doesn't frighten the orderly as much. And the doctor examines him with a sort of benevolence and satisfaction. That's a good cure!

Yes, Adrian is cured; he recovers consciousness; he asks for a mirror and one is presented to him. But he utters a cry of horror.

His beard!

His beard has been shaved off. The wretches!

He throws away the mirror. Why has his beard been shaved? They no longer like patients in hospitals to keep their beards. Hygienic concerns. Too many bacilli can cling on within them. Stupidities!

Adrian's fists clench, his eyes become bloodshot, his mouth vomits insults, One crisis more.

And he feels himself brutalized, wrapped up in he knows not what, which must be a straitjacket.

And more weeks go by, so long, so similar...

But here is the sun again. Winter is over. The tree has no leaves but buds are swelling there, impatient to unfold their marvels, and a bird is singing in its branches.

How pretty it is, that bird! It sings, its neck tilted back, its eyes dazzled, like that French goldfinch, which seemed to be gargling azure in a cage, and which is dead.

Adrian extends his arms toward the sun, the tree and the bird. Will he never get out of this hospital? Will he never be able to go and see what has become of Eve?

Oh, yes! Soon, he will go. He will eat so well, obey the doctor and the sun and everyone so meekly. They will let him go before the leaves have grown on that tree, He has to, for Eve, poor Eve,

What must she think, if she is alive? She has no communication with her Master, naturally, since he is not dead. And then she doubts, becomes discouraged, imagines that she is mistaken. She persuades herself that the soul is mortal, like the body, that spiritualism is a lie, the new religion a fraud.

Oh, to go and undeceive Eve! To tell her the truth, to render her faith, quickly!

Finally, on the eve of Easter, they believed that he was cured, and his *exeat* was given to him. What joy! His eyes recovered the clarity of fine days.

As his garments were filthy, and not very warm, he received the gift of a woolen cardigan and an overcoat. And he was given twenty francs, like a pauper.

He accepted, like a pauper. He did not have a sou. If he still had a few banknotes in his pockets on the evening of his suicide, his rescuers had probably stolen them.

He was grateful, like a pauper, for all those liberalities. But, interrogated one last time, he refused to reveal his name, to betray his dear secret, until the day when Eve could be informed. But he promised himself that he would soon make a donation of twenty thousand francs to that Spanish hospital in recognition of the good care that he had been given.

He left. The bells were ringing over the town, announcing the Resurrection: the bells of Spain, so fervent and so numerous.

He asked the way to the station, bought a third class ticked to Hendaye and boarded the first train that was going to France.

He was at the frontier before midday.

At the station buffet he drank some soup, ate a small loaf of bread and perfumed his mouth with an orange. The weather was fine. The summits had their blue robe.

At half past two, a new train deposited him at the station of Saint-Jean-de-Luz.

He had decided to stay there. All things considered, it was better not to present himself to Eve immediately—for he did not want to admit that she was dead, or even ill. Such an abrupt return, such an unexpected reappearance, might have overwhelmed her. It would be preferable to go to Ciboure first and present himself to Monsieur Bastarrèche, the worthy customs officer, the president of the spiritualist group. Once informed, that man would go to La Floride and prepare Eve, gradually, with all sorts of precautions and gradations, to receive the extraordinary visit. Yes, that was the best thing to do.

And Adrian immediately headed for Ciboure.

He was radiant. He smiled at the Easter sun, the buds on the willows, the scintillations of the Nivelle, which seemed and immense flow of precious stones, no longer a simple river of pure water, but a river of diamonds that the Basque mountains, generous lovers, were offering to the sea.

Easter. Alleluias. Renewals. Flowerings...

"Tomorrow, Eve, you will be happy," Adrian said, almost aloud, as he sought, through the side-streets of Ciboure, the house of the old customs man, those banal lodgings with the smell of frying and the shadows, frequented by the inhabitants of the stars.

XV. The Divine Illusion

Dr. Adrian knocked once, and twice. The door remained closed.

Then he knocked as of old: three raps first, then two, then one: the spiritualists' signal.

The door opened by a crack, and it was Monsieur Bastarrèche himself, the worthy customs officer, the president of the group, who appeared on the threshold. His face, with the twisted mouth and the unequal eyes, seemed even more worm-eaten, and his bony body, drier than a yule-log, gave the impression of an impending torch.

"Bonjour, Monsieur Bastarrèche."

"Bonjour, Monsieur."

"How are you? You don't recognize me?"

"No, I confess…"

"Come on, look at me carefully! It's true that I no longer have my beard…Adrian! Dr. Adrian!"

The eyes of the customs officer bulged. "Adrian?" he muttered, incredulously. And he took a step back, as if from a phantom.

"Well, yes, Adrian, who isn't dead. You thought he was dead, didn't you?"

"But…?"

"Well, he's alive. He's still alive. What a story! If you knew…"

"Oh, great God! Adrian!" repeated the customs man, blinking with stupor. "Is it possible?"

"Alas, yes."

"But…but…but…"

The customs officer put out his hand, felt the arm of the man who presented himself under the name of Adrian and who did, in fact, have the appearances of Adrian. Monsieur Bastarrèche would rather have believed in a psychic materialization than a veritable human individual, but a materialization in broad daylight, in the street...

"Is it possible?" he said, again, his legs giving way.

And he stood there, immobile, forgetting to invite that living form to cross the threshold, to come and sit down. Was it not about to dissolve like an astral body, an ephemeral perispirit, in a vapor?

"Will you have the kindness to let me in for a few minutes, my dear president. I'll tell you...what a pitiful adventure! It's this way, isn't it?"

Adrian turned right, toward the dining room, the well-known room in which he had so often taken part in spiritualist séances with Eve.

"But first, tell me Monsieur Bastarrèche, how is Mademoiselle Eve?"

"She's very well."

"Oh, praise God! She's not suffering?"

"No."

"So much the better! Do you see her sometimes?"

"Yesterday evening, again, here."

"She came to your home yesterday evening?"

"Yes, as I have the honor of telling you."

"So much the better, so much the better. And her morale, how is it?"

"Perfect."

"What must she think of me?"

"She believes you to be dead."

"Naturally. And you too, undoubtedly, believed that I was dead?"

"Well..."

"Well, my poor friend, I'm still alive, as you see, and I've come to offer you my apologies. What events! I'll explain to you..."

In the obscure dining-room, where a little lamp with red glass revealed a recent conversation with the spirits, Adrian took a chair, facing the customs man, and embarked upon a detailed recitation of his adventure.

"My dear president, Mademoiselle Eve must have told you how I threw myself into the sea one night in Spain?"

"Indeed."

"Well, I was pulled out of the water in spite of myself. I was unconscious. Fishermen picked me up in their boat. They were passing through the area. They saved me, unknown to me. They transported me to their home, in Saint Sébastien. And as no one knew who I was, and as my condition seemed grave, they deposited me at the hospital. And I stayed in that hospital until this morning—more than seven months. I nearly died for good. I was ill, I was mad...yes, mad, with a straitjacket. Astonishing! So many setbacks, so much anguish! The bad blood I created! But as soon as I could, I escaped and came to you. And here I am."

"My poor dear Monsieur!"

"Oh, you're right to pity me! You know, don't you? Mademoiselle Eve must have told you for what motives I wanted to kill myself?"

"In order to communicate with her after your death."

"That's right."

"To convince the incredulous. To demonstrate that the soul survives and that it can manifest itself to the living."

"That's it, precisely. And how disappointed you must have been, my dear president, and how disappointed Mademoiselle Eve must have been, on observing that you had no news of me!"

"But we have!" replied the customs man, bitterly.

Adrian went pale.

"What!" he cried. "You've had news of me?"

"Yes. We've had your writing, your messages, your apports."

"What!"

"You've appeared to us."

"Me?"

"Yes. Here. I've seen you there, in front of that curtain. I've seen you with my own eyes. We've all seen you, several times."

"Oh!"

"We had only to put the medium in a trance, and you appeared to us, you spoke to us."

"Me? Me?"

"Yes, you."

"But I'm not dead!"

"No, since here you are."

"But that's frightful."

"Indeed."

"That proves that we're mistaken, that we've always been dupes."

"I fear so."

"It proves that everything in the spiritualist doctrine is false; that there's nothing in it but illusions, childishness, inanities."

"I fear so."

"Oh my God! Why am I not dead! It would still be possible to believe!"

Adrian fell silent and lowered his head, his shoulders curbed, as if the heavens had collapsed upon him.

So, it was to arrive at this result that he had labored so hard, that he had turned that young woman away from natural paths, that he had prevented her from being a wife and mother, that he had stolen her from her relatives and society, that he had introduced an adventuress into La Floride, that he had driven Monsieur Illiberri to debauchery, to scandal, perhaps to ruination and dishonor. It was for this that he had been virtuous, sober and chaste! For this that he had suffered and caused suffering! For this that he had rejected Eve's kiss! For this!"

He stood up abruptly, and his eyes filled with tears.

"It's too terrible!" he cried. "It's impossible. I see my Hell. Everything will be explained. You've been the victim of an illusion, you, Eve and your friends. You've believed that it was me, but it wasn't me. It was some facetious spirit that took my form. It's someone who resembled me, but wasn't me. What made you believe that it was me?"

"But your face, your voice, your writing…our medium spoke like you, he had your ideas, your accent."

"What accent? I've never had an accent."

"But yes, Monsieur—the Parisian accent."

"Fifteen or twenty million people have that like me, the Parisian accent."

"But your fashion of writing? The *t*s crossed like yours, the final *s*s falling away like yours; Mademoiselle Eve even called attention, on the slate to the conjunctions, the *and*s, traced in the Elseverian fashion, like yours."

"But that's infernal!"

"She constantly has messages from you, Mademoiselle Eve. She's in communication with you in her orchard, in her bedroom, in her house. Everywhere that she summons you, you arrive. So?"

"And I speak to her like a dead man, like a disincarnate spirit?"

"Absolutely. You've told us about the sufferings of your dying, the impressions that you had in penetrating into the Afterlife."

"And have I told you where I was, in what part of the Afterlife?"

"Not me—but you have let Mademoiselle Eve understand, it appears, that you were on Jupiter."

"That's insane!"

"Mademoiselle Eve believes that she is with you constantly. Your perispirit never quits her. Ten times a day, she feels your breath on her eyes, your hands in hers."

"My God! And it will be necessary to undeceive her!"

"That's not all. The newspapers have announced your suicide, revealing the reasons that drive you to it. A heap of articles have been written on that subject, in Bayonne, in Paris and in London. Your book has appeared…"

"*Arrival in the Stars?*"

"Yes, *Arrival in the Stars*."

"What derision!"

"And it's a great success. One of our former collaborators completed it with the notes you left, and composed a final chapter with the documents furnished by Mademoiselle Eve."

"What documents?"

"Those she wrote after your disappearance, under your dictation."

"My God! Under my dictation!"

"And everyone finds it sublime. They're in the process of raising a statue to you."

"To me?"

"Exactly. Fifteen or twenty thousand francs have already been subscribed. England and America have given a great deal. Adhesions come from all directions. The spiritualist doctrine is propagating. Official scientists are studying it. Religions are adopting it. Recently, a French bishop, for the first time, had let it be understood that the phenomena might not be the work of Satan, and has agreed to study them with an open mind. You see what progress we're making?"

"It's incredible."

"And there's something else. Mademoiselle Eve has created, with her personal fortune—an inheritance from her mother, it's said—a Bureau Adrian."

"What's that?"

"A spiritualist agency, based in Bordeaux, which has the purpose of putting the living in communication with the dead."

"Oh, yes! Something like Julia's Bureau, in England?"

"That's it exactly."

"I did, in fact, mention that bureau to Mademoiselle Eve. And she's given it the name of the Bureau Adrian?"

"Yes, Monsieur, in memory of you."

"But that's frightful! She's perfectly convinced, then, herself?"

"How could she not be? She's just bought the house at Larbouset where you lived."

"Oh?"

"And she's retired there. She lives there, all alone."

"Poor friend!"

"She's in the process of creating a spiritualist library."

"Poor dear friend! And I'm going to prove to her that all that is false, absurd, ridiculous!"

"Oh, Monsieur, your false suicide, I can tell you, is a catastrophe! What will people think of us? What can we think of ourselves? Oh, it's enough to make one smash one's had against that wall! I, who believed so firmly…how paltry we are!"

Silence fell again. The two old men remained prostrate, confused, facing one another. And a beam of sunlight that passed between them, obliquely, seemed to cast gold on their misery.

From the direction of the staircase the old she-cat miaowed amorously. They could hear, in the distance, the impact of skittles and the sounds of drinkers. sometimes, the laughter of a tickled young woman rose up from an inn like an ardent rocket. Oh, the worthy creatures! How right they were, all of them, to be amorous, to be cheerful, to please themselves on this globe and not give themselves cricks in the neck gazing at the stars.

"Can I offer you something to drink?" asked the old customs man, humbly. And there was an indescribably pitiful abdication in his words, a resigned return to the poor things of this world.

"No, thank you," said Adrian, whose eyes became fulgurant again beneath their bushy eyebrows.

And after a long meditation, he said to his colleague: "Don't worry, Monsieur Bastarrèche. The catastrophe won't occur. I've reflected hard. I'm going to throw myself in the sea again, and this time, I'll take precautions to make sure I'm not pulled out again."

"Oh, my dear Monsieur, I'd be desolate if…."

"Don't be sorry. You're right. My false suicide would be a catastrophe. It won't be false."

"But it would be frightful, though…and my conscience…"

"You'll tranquilize it. Tell me, has anyone in your house perceived my return?"

"No, of course not."

"No one has been able to see me, to recognize me?"

"I don't think so. In any case, clean-shaven as you are, since I…"

"That's true."

"Then again, I'm alone in the house. Today, Easter Sunday, my daughter and my granddaughter have gone for a walk and the maid has gone out too."

"Well, render me the service, my dear friend, of not mentioning my visit to anyone, neither to your family nor to your servant, Don't mention it either to your friends the spiritualists or, above all, to Mademoiselle Eve. Will you promise?"

"I promise."

"Will you give me your word of honor?"

"You have it, Monsieur."

"Thank you."

"But I hope that you won't abuse it…but committing some irreparable action?"

"Have no fear. I have a clear vision of my duty, and I shall fulfill it. My friend, I believe that we were wrong to alarm ourselves just now. We have been deceived. What does that prove? Others are not? Conscientious scholars affirm that survival is real, that the souls of the dead come back to us, that we can see them and hear them in certain determined conditions. Let us believe, like them, in spite of everything!

"The phenomena that have been produced in my regard are doubtless explicable by autosuggestion, by telepathy, by the thousand artifices of the unconscious. You have all thought me dead and your belief must have forged the images, the sounds and the signs that represent me. That's already the proof that thought is creative, that the Word creates the world every day, that the abstract can make the concrete, that imagination is sometimes equivalent to reality. And is that not admirable?

"No, my dear friend, don't be discouraged. Work, study, seek as if you had not seen me today. But surround yourself, in your research, with all guarantees, all desirable sincerities. Check your mediums. Obtain others. See whether they do not contradict one another. Insure yourself against imposture. And continue bravely. Mademoiselle Eve has faith; it would be criminal to take it away from her. Let us leave her with the illusion, the necessary and divine illusion. Without that, what would our lives be worth?

"Mademoiselle Eve has faith and will serve to communicate it to others. To judge by what you have told me, she will probably create a school of psychic studies and devote her fortune to unveiling the Mystery. I don't want to annihilate such fine efforts. She will doubtless hasten the advent of the Truth. Thanks to her, it will be pursued with more ardor, more confidence, until it is discovered. And we shall end up making the division between what is real and what is false. The psychic sciences will progress, the light will burst forth...

"My friend, on high, where I hope to survive even so, I shall be happy. Adieu, then. And forever, this time. Will you permit me to embrace you? I have your word of honor that Mademoiselle Eve will know nothing of this, don't forget that. Love her well, in honor of me.

Always help her and comfort her. Is it not here that she ordinarily places her hands?"

He pointed to the edge of the table—the one that the sunlight had just quit.

"Yes," replied Monsieur Bastarrèche. "Yesterday, her hands were placed there."

"Thank you," said Adrian.

And his lips kissed the warm spot.

His eyes misted slightly. He walked to the door, supporting himself on the chairs. Then he parted the door-curtain, waved a last adieu with his hand, and disappeared, like a phantom, behind the cloth, behind which so many phantoms had disappeared.

XVI. The Great All and the Petty Nothing

Adrian went away like a rolling pebble along the sloping side-street and arrived at the harbor of Saint-Jean-de-Luz.

His visionary eyes no longer seemed to accord their gaze to the things around him. They were already turned toward the other side of life.

However, he perceived a solitary fisherman, reminiscent of a motionless heron on the edge of a pond.

He asked him: "Do you hire out boats?"

"Yes, Monsieur," the man replied.

"I'd like to take an excursion out to sea, on my own."

"Well, come this way. This is what you need.""

"How much?"

"A hundred sous an hour."

"Here's ten francs."

"Should I accompany you, Monsieur?"

"No need. Here, I'll add two francs. Will you lend me that rope?"

"As you wish. You'll be able to take it out of the harbor?"

"I hope so."

Adrian descended into the boat, took the oars and maneuvered. He was able to get out of the harbor, but it took a long time.

The water was blue, the town pink, the evening gilded.

It had been fifteen years since Adrian had touched an oar, and his recent illness had left him very anemic. He soon reduced his speed.

At Saint-Jean-de-Luz all the rowers head toward the dyke, but he commenced by going along the coast, attentive examining the stones on the shore.

He ended up discovering, at the foot of a fracture cliff, an oblong fragment of rock, rugged and heavy. He went to fetch it and carried it to his boat. It was hard work. It weighed a good twenty kilos.

Then he rowed toward the dyke, the long flat wall that forms the bay of Saint-Jean-de-Luz.

It took him half an hour to reach it.

The sea was splashing, drunk on the evening. The town was swooning in the setting sun. There were glorious windows in the houses, which threw off flames like the pupils of sated lovers.

In the distance, the earth was fuming, the mountains exalting. There was one that retained a little pink snow between two peaks, and a kiss of the heavens must have been placed there.

And the squeals of children rose up from the renewed greenery of a garden; excited dogs were pursuing one another along the beach. A frenetic automobile on a road left behind a wake of dust and frivolity.

Oh Life! Holy and magnificent and inexpressible Life!

Adrian gazed at all those things: the town and the mountain, the sea and the sky. And he breathed in deeply, as if to draw the soul of all that into his lungs.

He dropped the oars and put his hands together. The hour was so sweet! Unable to love, he wanted to pray.

And his prayer must have been something like this:

Great Master of All, who are everywhere, I don't know anything about you, and you have heard me groaning in that ignorance, and have left me therein. Forgive me! I have confidence in you. All that you have done is just, and the shadow into which you have plunged us is good. Light you will grant us, one day, when we have eyes strong enough to support it, and a heart great enough to contain it.

Great Master of All, you have given us a visual apparatus so paltry that we cannot reach the depths of anything around us, neither the great things nor the petty things, neither the stars that circle in the sky nor the worlds that stir in a grain of sand.

You have constructed our brain of materials so poor that we are unable to conceive either whether the infinite exists or whether it does not exist. You have surrounded us with obscure barriers against which we bruise ourselves as soon as we try to knock them down.

Well, Great Master of All, give us the wisdom to respect them, and to maintain ourselves, very humbly, within the narrow circle in which you have placed us.

If you have refused us organs powerful enough to discover what is happening in the stars, it is because nothing good can yet descend upon us from those heights. Let us therefore not attempt to scale them.

Since you have not constructed a visible gangway between the living and the dead, let us not try to cross that gulf. When we have glimpsed the piles of the bridge looming up, we can then attempt the passage.

Since our senses have been created for the earth alone, extinguish within us the desire for forbidden spheres.

Great Master of All, we shall remain in your shadow, meekly, patiently, until the evening when, having perfected ourselves sufficiently, purified ourselves sufficiently, you will take us by the hand to lead us toward the Light.

Great Master of All, your priests inform us that we shall be summoned to appear before you and that, in accordance with our actions, we shall be plunged into eternal delights or inextinguishable flames. Give us the wisdom to respect that information, since it is sufficient for our conscience, to believe in that religion, since is renders some of us better than others. Let us allow the unfortunate to hope, however puerile their hopes might be. Let us not break the old torches, even when they only illuminate empty palaces.

Great Master of All, I confide my nothing to you.

Adrian collected himself. The waves played with his boat. The breeze that brushed his hair had a sisterly tenderness.

"Great Master of All, will I have the strength to die?" he asked, raising his hands.

He wept. He gazed at the sun, which was shredding a cloud on the horizon and casting its shreds into the sea, like a rose from which plucks the petals in the bosom of a lover. He gazed at the violet mountains, which attracted feeble cirrus clouds from the depths of the valleys, as if for nocturnal kisses.

Amour! Over everything, Amour!

There was not a bubble of air, a flake of foam, a grain of dust, that was not impregnated with amour.

They were sighs of amour, those distant mists rising from the meadows; they were spasms of amour, the flux and reflux of the waves harassing the cliffs. And suddenly, from the center of the town, a silver bell-tower, beating like a heart, seemed to ask, with its grumbling bell:

"And you, what have you made of Amour?"

Through his tears, Dr. Adrian saw the entire landscape deformed, discolored, abolished. There were no longer waves, nor mountains, nor sky. There was...what?

There was that of which his heart and his brain had been full for such a long time, that which his thought summoned with so much violence. It was Eve. There was no longer anything but Eve around him, since there was nothing but Eve within him. Everything became her. The universe resolved itself into her.

A hallucination? Perhaps. The materialization of a dream, a desire, and amour—the more brilliant and the saddest amour? Surely. To his psychic appeal she came, as real as a mistress if flesh, punctual at a rendezvous.

She was there, arms open. And the blonde dusk, which was beginning to spread over the earth, was her blonde hair flowing over him. She really was there, loving him, forgiving him, thanking him. And via the angelus bell, she must have been saying to him:

What have you made of me? The happiest of women, the most passionate of lovers, who will never forget you, and whose atoms will disintegrate still crying thank you *to you, my love.*

You have left me the illusion, you have left me purity. May the Great Master of all thank you, my love.

If you had only loved me with a terrestrial amour, I would have seen my happiness crumble after a few months. But you have honored me with a supernatural amour and my happiness will traverse the centuries, my love.

I shall be happy, in all those happy people that you will make; in those desperate mothers who are afraid of being unable to rejoin their sons through the stone of the tomb, in those tormented thinkers who dreaded that their genius would not survive their putrefaction. My heart will love you in their hearts, my love.

People have thought you mad, and perhaps you have been. But what is a madman? A hallucinated indi-

vidual, an independent individual who detaches himself from the flock in the process of trampling through the undergrowth and who boldly seeks a new route, all alone, toward splendid horizons. You have searched; someone will find, my love.

"Thanks to you and the discoveries that you will provoke, there will be a little more hope among the dolorous crowds that an obtuse materialism has deprived of all hope. And that is why what you call your nothing *will be warmly welcomed by the Great All.*

Go, go! Do your superb work" You can throw your corpse into the depths of the sea; your soul will go to the stars, my love,

My love, my love!

The bell had fallen silent.

"My love!" cried Dr. Adrian, his arms open.

And he blew a long kiss to the dusk.

Then he attached one of the ends of the rope to the fragment of rock, knotted the other end around his neck, picked up the whole in his hands, leaned over the edge of the boat, dived, and disappeared.

A few brief bubbles on the somber sea might have been an indication of the last breath of a great philosopher, or of a tiny fish playing beneath the surface.

SF & FANTASY

André Couvreur. *Caresco, Superman; The Exploits of Professor Tornada* (3 vols.); *The Necessary Evil*
Gaston Danville. *The Perfume of Lust*
Camille Debans. *The Misfortunes of John Bull*
Captain Danrit. *Undersea Odyssey*
C. I. Defontenay. *Star (Psi Cassiopeia)*
Charles Derennes. *The People of the Pole*
Georges Dodds (anthologist). *The Missing Link*
Charles Dodeman. *The Silent Bomb*
Harry Dickson. *The Heir of Dracula; Harry Dickson vs. The Spider*
Jules Dornay. *Lord Ruthven Begins*
Alfred Driou. *The Adventures of a Parisian Aeronaut*
Odette Dulac. *The War of the Sexes*
Alexandre Dumas. *The Return of Lord Ruthven; The Man who Married a Mermaid* (w/P. Lacroix)
Renée Dunan. *Baal; The Ultimate Pleasure*
J.-C. Dunyach. *The Night Orchid; The Thieves of Silence*
Henri Duvernois. *The Man Who Found Himself*
Achille Eyraud. *Voyage to Venus*
Henri Falk. *The Age of Lead*
Paul Féval. *Anne of the Isles; Knightshade; Revenants; Vampire City; The Vampire Countess; The Wandering Jew's Daughter*
Paul Féval, *fils. Felifax, the Tiger-Man*
Charles de Fieux. *Lamékis*
Fernand Fleuret. *Jim Click*
Charles-Marie Flor O'Squarr. *Phantoms*
Louis Forest. *Someone is Stealing Children in Paris*
Arnould Galopin. *Doctor Omega; Doctor Omega and the Shadowmen* (anthology)
Judith Gautier. *Isoline and the Serpent-Flower*
H. Gayar. *The Marvelous Adventures of Serge Myrandhal on Mars*
Louis Geoffroy. *The Apocryphal Napoleon*
G.L. Gick. *Harry Dickson and the Werewolf of Rutherford Grange*
Raoul Gineste. *The Second Life of Doctor Albin*
Delphine de Girardin. *Balzac's Cane*
Léon Gozlan. *The Vampire of the Val-de-Grâce*
Jules Gros. *The Fossil Man*
Jimmy Guieu. *The Polarian-Denebian War* (2 vols.)
Edmond Haraucourt. *Daah, the First Human; Illusions of Immortality*
Nathalie Henneberg. *The Green Gods*
Eugène Hennebert. *The Enchanted City*

Jules Hoche. *The Maker of Men and His Formula*
V. Hugo, P. Foucher & P. Meurice. *The Hunchback of Notre-Dame*
Romain d'Huissier. *Hexagon: Dark Matter*
Jules Janin. *The Magnetized Corpse*
Gustave Kahn. *The Tale of Gold and Silence*
Gérard Klein. *The Mote in Time's Eye*
Fernand Kolney. *Love in 5000 Years*
Paul Lacroix. *Danse Macabre; The Man who Married a Mermaid* (w/Alexandre Dumas)
Louis-Guillaume de La Follie. *The Unpretentious Philosopher*
Jean de La Hire. *The Fiery Wheel; Enter the Nyctalope; The Nyctalope on Mars; The Nyctalope vs. Lucifer; The Nyctalope Steps In; Night of the Nyctalope; Return of the Nyctalope*
Etienne-Léon de Lamothe-Langon. *The Virgin Vampire*
André Laurie. *Spiridon*
Gabriel de Lautrec. *The Vengeance of the Oval Portrait*
Alain le Drimeur. *The Future City*
Georges Le Faure & Henri de Graffigny. *The Extraordinary Adventures of a Russian Scientist Across the Solar System* (2 vols.)
Gustave Le Rouge. *The Dominion of the World* (w/Gustave Guitton) (4 vols.); *The Mysterious Doctor Cornelius* (3 vols.); *The Vampires of Mars*
Jules Lermina. *The Battle of Strasbourg; Mysteryville; Panic in Paris; The Secret of Zippelius; To-Ho and the Gold Destroyers*
Maurice Level. *The Gates of Hell*
André Lichtenberger. *The Centaurs; The Children of the Crab*
Maurice Limat. *Mephista*
Listonai. *The Philosophical Voyager*
Jean-Marc & Randy Lofficier. *Edgar Allan Poe on Mars; The Katrina Protocol; Pacifica 1, 2; Robonocchio; Return of the Nyctalope;* (anthologists) *Tales of the Shadowmen 1-13; The Vampire Almanac* (2 vols.)
Ch. Lomon & P.-B. Gheuzi. *The Last Days of Atlantis*
Camille Mauclair. *The Virgin Orient*
Xavier Mauméjean. *The League of Heroes*
Joseph Méry. *The Tower of Destiny*
Hippolyte Mettais. *Paris Before the Deluge; The Year 5865*
Louise Michel. *The Human Microbes; The New World*
Tony Moilin. *Paris in the Year 2000*
Michael Moorcock's *Legends of the Multiverse*
José Moselli. *Illa's End*

John-Antoine Nau. *Enemy Force*

Marie Nizet. *Captain Vampire*

Charles Nodier. *Trilby and The Crumb Fairy*

C. Nodier, A. Beraud & Toussaint-Merle. *Frankenstein*

Henri de Parville. *An Inhabitant of the Planet Mars*

Gaston de Pawlowski. *Journey to the Land of the 4th Dimension*

Georges Pellerin. *The World in 2000 Years*

Ernest Pérochon. *The Frenetic People*

Pierre Pelot. *The Child Who Walked on the Sky*

Jean Petithuguenin. *An International Mission to the Moon*

J. Polidori, C. Nodier, E. Scribe. *Lord Ruthven the Vampire*

P.-A. Ponson du Terrail. *The Immortal Woman; The Vampire and the Devil's Son; The Police Agent*

Georges Price. *The Missing Men of the* Sirius

René Pujol. *The Chimerical Quest*

Edgar Quinet. *Ahasuerus; The Enchanter Merlin*

Henri de Régnier. *A Surfeit of Mirrors*

Maurice Renard. *The Blue Peril; Doctor Lerne; The Doctored Man; A Man Among the Microbes; The Master of Light*

Restif de la Bretonne. *The Discovery of the Austral Continent by a Flying Man; Posthumous Correspondence* (3 vols.); *The Fay Ouroucoucou* (2 vols.)

Jean Richepin. *The Crazy Corner; The Wing*

Albert Robida. *The Adventures of Saturnin Farandoul; Chalet in the Sky; The Clock of the Centuries; The Electric Life; The Engineer Von Satanas*

J.-H. Rosny Aîné. *Helgvor of the Blue River; The Givreuse Enigma; The Mysterious Force; The Navigators of Space; Vamireh; The World of the Variants; The Young Vampire*

Marcel Rouff. *Journey to the Inverted World*

Marie-Anne de Roumier-Robert. *The Voyage of Lord Seaton to the Seven Planets*

Léonie Rouzade. *The World Turned Upside Down*

Han Ryner. *The Human Ant; The Superhumans*

Louis-Claude de Saint-Martin. *The Crocodile*

Frank Schildiner. *The Quest of Frankenstein; The Triumph of Frankenstein*

Nicolas Ségur. *The Human Paradise*

Pierre de Selenes: *An Unknown World*

Norbert Sevestre. *Sâr Dubnotal: Vs. Jack the Ripper; The Astral Trail*

Angelo de Sorr. *The Vampires of London*

Brian Stableford. *The Empire of the Necromancers (1. The Shadow of Frankenstein; 2. Frankenstein and the Vampire Countess; 3. Frankenstein in London); The Wayward Muse; Eurydice's Lament; The Mirror of Dionysius; The New Faust at the Tragicomique; Sherlock Holmes and The Vampires of Eternity; The Stones of Camelot* (anthologist) *News from the Moon; The Germans on Venus; The Supreme Progress; The World Above the World; Nemoville; Investigations of the Future; The Conqueror of Death; The Revolt of the Machines; The Man With the Blue Face; The Aerial Valley; The New Moon; The Nickel Man; On the Brink of the World's End; The Mirror of Present Events; The Humanisphere*

Jacques Spitz. *The Eye of Purgatory*

Kurt Steiner. *Ortog*

Eugène Thébault. *Radio-Terror*

C.-F. Tiphaigne de La Roche. *Amilec*

Simon Tyssot de Patot. *The Strange Voyages of Jacques Massé and Pierre de Mésange*

Louis Ulbach. *Prince Bonifacio*

Théo Varlet. *The Castaways of Eros; The Golden Rock.; The Martian Epic* (w/Octave Joncquel); *Timeslip Troopers* (w/André Blandin); *The Xenobiotic Invasion*

Pierre Véron. *The Merchants of Health*

Paul Vibert. *The Mysterious Fluid*

Villiers de l'Isle-Adam. *The Scaffold; The Vampire Soul*

Gaston de Wailly. *The Murderer of the World*

Philippe Ward. *Artahe; Manhattan Ghost* (w/Mickael Laguerre); *The Song of Montségur* (w/Sylvie Miller)

Victor Margueritte. *The Bacheloress; The Companion; The Couple*